ENCOURAGEMENT ENOUGH

Did he just open the door and enter? Or knock and wait for permission? Or should he even go into her room? Theo had bought her time, but he had also presented her to the innkeep as a respectable lady, and he was loath to do anything that might get them both tossed from the inn. He didn't fancy a night without a soft mattress under him.

Of course, if he could have something else soft underneath him, it might be worth it.

The image of Molly's lush figure pulled a smile from him and gave him encouragement enough. For the last five miles in the carriage, she had been brushing up against him—a touch of her shoulder against his, a rub of her cheek before she jerked upright, and even one sweet stroke of her breast against his arm. And he'd been unable to do anything since he had his hands full with four reins and two horses.

Not what a fellow really wanted to hold, blast it.

BOOK YOUR PLACE ON OUR WEBSITE AND MAKE THE READING CONNECTION!

We've created a customized website just for our very special readers, where you can get the inside scoop on everything that's going on with Zebra, Pinnacle and Kensington books.

When you come online, you'll have the exciting opportunity to:

- View covers of upcoming books
- Read sample chapters
- Learn about our future publishing schedule (listed by publication month *and author*)
- Find out when your favorite authors will be visiting a city near you
- Search for and order backlist books from our online catalog
- Check out author bios and background information
- Send e-mail to your favorite authors
- Meet the Kensington staff online
- Join us in weekly chats with authors, readers and other guests
- Get writing guidelines
- AND MUCH MORE!

Visit our website at
http://www.kensingtonbooks.com

A PROPER MISTRESS

Shannon Donnelly

ZEBRA BOOKS
Kensington Publishing Corp.
http://www.kensingtonbooks.com

ZEBRA BOOKS are published by

Kensington Publishing Corp.
850 Third Avenue
New York, NY 10022

All Kensington titles, imprints and distributed lines are avail-
able at special quantity discounts for bulk purchases for sales
promotion, premiums, fund-raising, educational or institu-
tional use.

Special book excerpts or customized printings can also be
created to fit specific needs. For details, write or phone the
office of the Kensington Special Sales Manager: Kensington
Publishing Corp., 850 Third Avenue, New York, NY 10022.
Attn. Special Sales Department. Phone: 1-800-221-2647.

Zebra and the Z logo Reg. U.S. Pat. & TM Off.

First Printing: May 2003
10 9 8 7 6 5 4 3 2 1

Printed in the United States of America

For Marsha
May you always find the courage
to choose happiness

One

"Beauty ain't required, but she's got to catch the eye," Theodore Winslow said, striding across the small salon, one hand fisted behind his back and the other gesturing in the air. "I mean, I'm supposed to be smitten. But she can't be at all acceptable—only she can't be too coarse, either, mind. My father would twig to it at once. No, she must have manners enough that hanging out for the respectability of marriage seems obvious. And it would be best if she had red hair—m'family knows I've a weakness for red hair. But I'll leave that detail to you."

"Red hair," Sallie Ellis repeated, her tone thoughtful.

Theo turned from the window that overlooked the small, quiet square near Covent Garden. Was he making a mull of it? Sallie had a rather calculating look in her bright, blue eyes. A look he'd come to know a good deal about of late. Between his dealings with the temperamental Antonia and the greedy Davina, he'd seen more than he ever wanted to of that look.

But this was not his last hope. No, if Sallie named a sum beyond reason, he would simply walk out. He would, indeed. Only the pressure of time passing nibbled at his heels. He'd had that terse note from his father nearly a week ago: Had the squire acted on his threat already? Well, if he had, he'd just have to unmake his will again. He frowned. Law wasn't his strong suit, but he was certain wills could be made and unmade. To be on the safe side, however, he would waste as little time as possible, a course that better suited him anyway. Blazes, did he hate waiting.

"'Course, I'm fond enough of blondes as well," he added. There, that should widen the field and bit and keep the price within means. One had to pay for being too particular. He had learned that lesson years ago when buying his first hunter.

"Mmmmmmmm," Sallie said, now tapping one finger against her plump and powdered cheek. For a woman past her prime, she still had a round enough figure to be easy on a man's eye, Theo thought. Yes, nice curves that a fellow would enjoy having his hands around, and a dimple in her right cheek. But those shrewd, assessing eyes of hers left him wary.

Theo glanced around the room again, eyeing the red velvet drapery and the red damask hung on the walls. Rather rich looking, he thought. Cream-painted wainscoting kept the room from overpowering, but those sticks of furniture and vases and whatnots had the look of having cost ridiculous sums.

And was Sallie now calculating how much she could raise her usual rates? Well, at least he could admire the paintings in the room while he waited—lovely nude women in all of them, with bits of classical white drapery at their heels. Heavens knew why a female could go dancing around in the altogether in ancient times, but not now. Must be that the weather had cooled off a touch.

Clearing his throat, Theo stretched his neck. His blasted neckcloth felt tight as a noose, though it had seemed fine this morning when he'd tied it at The Queen's Head Inn where he'd been staying since he'd got to London three days ago. He hoped he looked as cool a customer as ever stepped through Sallie Ellis's painted red doors. Trouble was, he wasn't at all accustomed to dealing for his women. Why should he, when he'd always been able to find a willing tavern wench, or a maid with a roving eye, or even a country girl with a flirting glint to her eyes? Women seemed to like him, though he didn't know why. He wasn't a patch on Terrance.

Still, he needed a certain type of female just now— one as could be hired, and he was done dealing with actresses. Lord, was he ever.

So he had made his way to Sallie Ellis. Terrance had recommended the establishment some time ago, in one of those bits of advice he had tossed at Theo over the years. "Good girls there," he'd said, his voice only a little slurred at the time from a night out with Theo. "Clean of body, and not of mind. And Sallie will give you a fair price."

Well, that part he wanted. As to how good the girls really were—well, he wanted one that wasn't too good. No, he had a feeling he would be better off with one more than a little bad.

Sallie had been staring up at a corner of the room as if she was trying to recall a name or a number. The longer she stared, the more Theo wanted to fidget. He rocked forward on his toes and back on the heels of his riding boots, wishing this was over.

It was Terrance's fault, of course. Most things were. Only he didn't hold Terrance to blame, really. No, Terrance was a good gun, a great fellow, the best of brothers, and very much the wronged party here.

But he did hold his father at fault for trying to manipulate him and Terrance yet again. And by heavens it stopped here and now.

Or it would as soon as he got home.

He gave a grim smile. He could hardly wait to see his father's face when he made his announcement.

"It is possible that I may have someone for you," Sallie said, her accent too carefully cultured to be natural for her. She put down the china tea cup and saucer that she had had in her lap. "However, you said you would need a gal for a week or more? Couldn't you make do with three days of her time?"

"Three days!" Theo said, his voice rising with outrage. "What, am I to gallop her to Somerset and back? Well, you may think again on that. I need her a week, perhaps more, and I've brought fifty guineas, with a hundred more to pay at the end of it. And that ought to buy well more than three days!"

Sallie's eyes widened and her accent slipped as she breathed, "Coo, that's a right nice bit of the ready."

Scowling, Theo pressed his lips tight. Devil a bit, but he should have waited for her to name a price. Still, she seemed to be rethinking herself now, and if he brought this off for the sum he named, he would be thankful. Davina had wanted four hundred guineas, after all. And for only four days. Actresses! He ought to have known their seeming concern for a fellow's plight always amounted to nothing more than a sham. That was their trade, after all. Far better to hire a woman whose trade was making a fellow honestly feel better.

Sallie still had not answered, so he asked, brow furrowed and already starting to wonder where he might try next, "But if you cannot spare a girl so long, I—"

"Now, now, Mr. Winslow, let us not be hasty," Sallie said, her accent again acquiring the smooth gloss of the upper class. "I consider it my duty to never let a gentleman leave my house unsatisfied. So let us put our heads together. Are you certain you could not make do with a brunette? No—I see by the look in your eyes, that would not do. You gentlemen are so particular about some details. But for such a long time . . . well, that does seem rather worth more than a hundred and fifty."

Theo stiffened. He had reached the end of his patience. "Well, I don't see how. It's a guaranteed sum, and who's to say she might otherwise sit idle here, not bringing you a penny!"

Sallie chuckled. "Oh, Mr. Winslow. My girls never sit idle, though they do lay around a bit." She laughed at her own coarse joke, and Theo tried to summon a smile, though he found himself rather offended by such vulgarity.

Devil a bit, if Sallie had a girl anything like herself, she'd be perfectly horrible. Just what he wanted, in fact.

A soft knock sounded on the door and a moment later a black pageboy in cream satin—turban, coat, and breeches—came in. He carried a note on a silver tray, balancing the tray in one hand, and holding the note down with the other. But when he reached Sallie, he took his hand off the note and offered the tray with a small, well-practiced bow.

"Your pardon, Mr. Winslow," Sallie said, taking up the note. "The business of pleasure is far from pleasure itself."

She waved a plump hand for the boy to go away, her rings flashing, and he bowed himself out as she tore open the note and scanned it. Then she rose with a shake of her gold satin skirts, those blue eyes of hers even more calculating, enough so that Theo found himself shifting uneasily from foot to foot.

"A trifle I must attend to, Mr. Winslow. Do help yourself to wine or brandy. I promise to be back in just a moment with perhaps a most excellent solution." She offered a brilliant smile, her teeth white and small, and the charm that had built this house swept over him, sweet as honeysuckle. It would, no doubt, become just as cloying over time, but for now, he found himself setting aside his doubts about her and grinning back, and wishing he had just a bit more time to spend here.

Lord, she was a rogue—and if she were twenty years younger, he'd hire her for the job. But it wouldn't do to bring home a ladybird his father's age. No, the squire would see through that in two seconds.

"Now, don't you slip away," Sallie said, wagging a finger at him.

With a flirtatious wink, she left, hips swaying enough to catch a gentleman's eye—Sallie prided herself that she knew all the tricks of her trade.

However, as soon as the door closed behind her, she pressed her back to it and glanced heavenwards. "Thank you," she said, the words heartfelt.

Here she'd been thinking just this morning she might not have the ready at hand to pay the rent on her townhouse this month, and had been cursing those girls of hers what had run off with that dratted Frenchman.

She ought to know better than to cater to the foreign trade, but he had flashed a fistful of banknotes and she had let her own rules slip. Business first, she taught her girls. Or tried to. And what did she get for not keeping to her own rules?—why, he had upped and run off with Bette and Jane, two of her best, leaving his bill unpaid as well. That's what she got! Gone off to Paris, Jane had said in the note she had left behind. All three of them. Why it wasn't even decent!

And without so much as a single day's notice.

In the normal course of things, it would not have mattered. She would have replaced those two within the month, for there seemed an endless supply of girls in London with foolish hopes and no skills to hire out but what God gave them.

Sallie shook her head. She had been one of those girls. But she'd learned. Oh, she had learned. And she tried to teach her girls well, too. Survival and success depended on a hard head and an even harder heart. But with two girls skittered off only just yesterday, and three more laid low by the influenza this past week, she had been looking at her books and fearing some of her jewels might have to go into hock before the end of the month. She gave a small shudder. Her jewels were her retirement, and she'd rather have a tooth pulled than be parted from so much as a single pearl. Once they started going, after all, no telling but what she might end up on the street.

And that wasn't for Sallie Ellis, mind!

But along comes this young gent with his ready money—and those lovely blue eyes of his.

She gave a small sigh. Oh, to be twenty again—or even thirty—and able to hire herself out. But she had given up that side of the business. Still, he could tempt any girl, what with that thick black hair of his, which did not seem to want to stay in place. She'd already guessed he'd strip as fine as any prize fighter she'd known—all that masculine long, hard muscle and broad shoulders. Oh, didn't she just have a weakness for a tall gentleman. And didn't he just have a mouth for kisses, all finely made and with that quirk at the side when he smiled. It'd be a lucky girl who had him for her job.

Sallie glanced at the note in her hand, mouth tightening. 'Course, odds were that Molly wouldn't see it that way. Of all the foolish things for a woman to have in a whorehouse, Molly had principles. Sallie gave a small snort. *Principles!* Well, when it came to keeping her house in style, Sallie had but one principle—her house came first.

So she fixed a smile in place and headed toward the kitchen.

She stopped as soon as she entered, entranced by the rush of enticing aromas—roasting meat, a heavenly mix of onion and curry from a simmering pot, the yeasty fragrance of baking bread. With it came the comfortable chatter of gossip passing to Molly from the between-maids.

Sallie smiled. It had been a lucky day indeed when she'd met up with Molly Sweet.

Painted a sunny yellow, the kitchen lay at the back of the house. Two sash windows and a door looked onto what was now a kitchen garden, where once there'd only been a square of grass. Molly's doing, that. A skylight had been set into the ceiling last year, making the room bright, and a silver chain hung down from it, to open the glass cover and cool the room.

In the far corner, copper pots hung from a circular iron rack that dangled from the tall ceiling. Shelves wound around the room, displaying china serving dishes as well as provisions, the only one of which Sallie could identify was the tall, white cone, ready to be scraped for sugar.

Underfoot, scrubbed stone floors gleamed a soft cream, and just now the room seemed crowded with bodies and noise. For a moment, Sallie frowned as she added up just how much Molly cost her in staff. A white-clad scullery maid sat on a three-legged stool, peeling potatoes. Another, also dressed in white—who also did for upstairs at times—rolled pastry out on the large, rectangular oak table in the center of the room. And young Alice—a girl not yet ten, who Sallie had found on the streets six months ago—stirred the steaming pot on the latest innovation, an enclosed brick stove.

The fireplace had also been put to use, roasting a joint of mutton. Robert, the black page boy, sat near the hearth, turning the spit, his turban gone and an apron over his satin coat and breeches. He stared at the meat as if already concentrated on his portion.

And watching all of this, poking into everything, was Molly.

Well, Molly's staff certainly cost a goodly sum, but Sallie had to admit that her cooking also brought in trade—and there weren't anything so generous as a man with *all* his needs met.

With her mouth starting to water from the assault of aromas, Sallie straightened and reminded herself of business. She hadn't gotten ahead, after all, by letting distractions deter her from her goals. So she glanced around once more, then said, a warm smile in place, "Molly, ducks, spare a minute will you?"

Turning from the table where she had been supervising the rolling out of pastry by the between-maid, Molly used the back of her hand to push away a red curl that had escaped her white cap, then she offered a flour-streaked smile. "Sallie, I hardly expected you so prompt. And I do beg pardon for intruding—I know you were with a gentleman, but I must talk to you about the tarts."

Sallie almost frowned. At fourteen, she had fled a Methodist upbringing, and at times it still seemed to her that Molly's endless smiles were more of a sin than anything else that went on in her house. It just wasn't . . . wasn't seemly for anyone to be so cheerful. Life was hard. Earnest. But after five years, she ought to be used to Molly always looking for sunshine, even on the darkest days.

So she stuffed down her irritation. "Yes, ducks, but the tarts can wait."

Molly gave a shake of her head. "That's just it—they cannot."

Sallie almost let out a sigh. What with her figure and hair, and that sweet voice of hers—quite the proper one, too—Molly could have made a fortune if she'd taken to the other side of business. But she'd had a proper upbringing before she'd been orphaned and abandoned to the world, and that showed in more than just her voice. Such a pity to waste her talents in a kitchen, of all the silly things!

Molly dusted the flour from her hands, onto her apron, as she came forward to explain her disaster. "Alice is just back from the market and there's not an apricot to be had—even though it is high summer. I know how particular Lord Alvanley is about them, but do you think we might get away with serving peach tarts instead, and just hope he does not bite into one? I mean, more than half the time, he just wants to see we have his favorite on the sideboard."

"Oh, bother the tarts, ducks. We've other business." Taking Molly's hand, Sallie pulled her from the kitchen.

"But the tarts must go in within the hour, or I'll never have time to finish the rest of the baking!"

"It'll wait," Sallie insisted, and then she stopped in the hallway and stood before Molly. She ran her stare down and then up Molly, tapping one finger against her cheek. For a moment, she hesitated at what she was about to do. But then she thought of the money—always a good thing to do. Yes, and she'd make it a fair share between them. Fair enough, at least. After all, she was the one who'd met the gentleman and had thought of Molly.

With a nod, she straightened. "The apron must come off. And the cap, too."

She suited actions to the words, snatching the white lace-trimmed cap as Molly sputtered a protest. Spinning the younger woman around, Sallie pulled loose the ties to Molly's plain, starched apron.

"What are you doing?" Molly said, a hand going up to push at her tumble of curls, and baffled by Sallie's actions.

It was Molly's one pride that her hair could shine like polished copper when brushed and arranged. But in a kitchen with open flames, long hair could be a dangerous asset. So she hadn't done more than tie up the long curls this morning and stuff her cap on, for she had slept late. Which is why her baking was not yet done.

And it seemed it might never get done today. Well, life was always interesting at Sallie's house.

Sallie's plump, stubby fingers closed on her shoulders and Molly allowed herself to be pulled around again. But when Sallie tossed apron and cap onto the floor, Molly snatched them back. "Really, now. What has gotten into you?"

"I want you to meet a gentleman."

Molly froze. Then her anger fired, sizzling through her and warming her skin. She'd thought this business settled at last between them, but it seemed it would never be.

"Sallie—" she started, her tone warning, but Sallie was already shaking her head and starting to lead her upstairs, an arm over her shoulders.

"It's not like that, ducks. He's not looking for a tumble. And he's got fifty pounds in his pocket—all just meant for you!"

"I do not care if he . . . fifty pounds?" Molly stuttered over the words as the sum registered. She did not care to think of herself as mercenary, but she had learned to be as practical as any girl in Sallie's house. And fifty pounds! Gracious, that deserved more than practicality. That sum merited full consideration.

Then her eyes narrowed. "Fifty pounds for what, exactly?"

"Nothing much. He just wants some fancy piece to act up a bit in front of his family—you know, carry on as if you're enamored of him. Why, you could consider it a holiday, almost. A paid one at that! I wouldn't ask, ducks, but then I thought to m'self, I thought, Sallie, why not just offer our own dear Molly a chance at some of the easiest money ever? You've been good enough to me, ducks, and I'd like to help you get that inn you talked about wanting so dearly."

Sallie grinned.

Molly hugged her apron and cap even tighter. It had been such a mistake to sip too much of that lovely sweet port Sallie had bought Christmas last. That was the one holiday when the house closed, and Molly had always delighted in fixing a proper feast for the girls. But last year, with the candles guttering low, and the smell of pine in the house, and the goose and ham and mincemeat pies and plum pudding eaten, she had sat with Sallie. And she had drunk too much and started to talk about her dream of an inn—a place where she could be mistress and make a respectable name for herself as a cook.

Oh, she never ought to have confided so much.

The next day Sallie had again suggested a means for Molly to double her income. And Sallie had not stopped offering persuasion until Molly had threatened to walk out. However, she knew—and Sallie did, as well—that her threat carried no real weight. Respectable London houses were not like to hire a cook whose only reference came from a house of ill-repute. And life in another house such as this might not prove so comfortable.

But Sallie had relented. At least, she had back then.

Chin raised, Molly fixed her employer with a firm stare. "What else does he want for his fifty pounds?"

Sallie started up the stairs again. "That's just it, ducks. He may have the ready at hand, but you have the goods he needs, so to speak. And what he needs is not a good time between the sheets, but a smart girl who can handle herself well—which means, you name the tune and he pays the piper!"

A shrewd look had come into Sallie's eyes as she spoke, and Molly knew she had been unwise to show any interest. How could she even think of hiring herself out to some stranger? She knew the answer, however. She still could remember what it had felt like at twelve to be cold, hungry and alone—and terrified. One could do anything, given the right circumstances.

So what would she do for fifty pounds?

She earned twenty pounds a year from Sallie, and with London prices being what they were, she managed to save but five or six pounds a year. Last year she had tucked away a solid nine pounds and sixpence. But with fifty pounds in hand, she would have enough that she could start to look for the inn she wanted.

Her own place.

Her thoughts spun faster and faster, imagining it.

Then they reached the landing on the first floor and stopped outside Sallie's best parlor.

"Look, ducks, I've always told you that keepin' company with any gentleman on a paying basis is safe as houses. Set the terms up front, and you can't go wrong. And all this gent wants is a gal who'll pretend to be his bride and mortify his family. That ain't much work for the kind of money he's offerin'."

Molly frowned. "Pretend to be a bride? That sounds a bit daft—or is this some sort of wager?" She might be the cook in a bawdy house, but even she knew that betting occupied a good deal of any fashionable gentleman's attention.

"He ain't touched, ducks." Sallie glanced behind her at the parlor door, then she looked back at Molly, her eyes sharp as shards of ice. "But you just look 'im over for yourself 'afore you make any final answer."

Suspicion chilled Molly's skin. Just what was Sallie plotting?

In truth, she would never call Sallie wicked. Sallie might have the morals of a London stray tabby and be as canny as one, but she had her own sort of code, odd as it was. Molly had never seen her offer any unkindness to any of her girls, and to be fair, she had never coerced any girl into service. From the tales the girls told of other houses, such consideration was not always the case. Still, Sallie had a sly look to her just now, as if she had not been completely honest.

But if she said the gentleman only wanted companionship, perhaps that was the case. And there was that lovely temptation of fifty pounds.

"Come on," Sally urged. "Just meet him at least. What's the harm in that?"

Molly took her lower lip between her teeth, and then glanced at the closed parlor door. That seemed to be all the hesitation Sallie needed, for she grabbed Molly's hand, saying, "I always knew you for a fly one."

Sallie might think her knowing, but right now she felt quite the opposite. Her chest tight, Molly asked, "Should I perhaps change my gown first?"

"Oh, he won't be looking at that, ducks. And don't you fret that he won't take to you—he's partial to redheads."

Molly's stomach gave a lurch as if she had just pulled a burning pie from her oven. Just after they had first met, Sallie had introduced another gentleman with a fondness for redheads to her—a florid-faced banker to whom Sallie had tried to sell Molly's favors. A few pungent words from Molly had changed his mind about his preference, and she'd had more words with Sallie until the shouting had gathered the attention of everyone in the house. After Molly had broken every vase in her room, and smashed one chair even, Sallie had agreed to Molly's terms that she work in the kitchen or not at all. They had gotten along very well on those terms since.

But now a tremor of apprehension fluttered into Molly at the thought of having to meet any gentleman in Sallie's house.

Then she thought of everything else she had been through in her life—the barely remembered early years in India, the long voyage home with her heart still grieving, that time alone in London when she knew not a single soul, and the hard life of the workhouse. She squared her shoulders. She had been through worse than this.

And hadn't her late uncle always told her: "A soldier stands fast, Molly-may."

She could still hear his gruff voice. He had certainly faced his own death brave enough, so to honor his memory she would face this gentleman.

After all, she had made no promise that she would agree to this preposterous bargain.

Still, she had to take a breath as Sallie pulled open the

gilt-edged door to the drawing room. Then she found her apron and cap plucked from her cold hands, and a hand pushing on the small of her back as Sallie whispered to her, "And if you don't think those are the loveliest blue eyes you've ever seen, you're blind, ducks."

With a firm shove, Sallie sent Molly into the room.

The gentleman turned from where he had been standing near the window and Molly blinked.

Gracious, those were indeed the loveliest eyes. Quite the most amazing shade of deep blue, like the sky at twilight. They stared at her with a startling intensity from a face that she had not expected either, and which had her blurting out the first words that came into her head.

"Why, you're hardly more than a boy yourself! Why ever do you want to go hiring a woman from this house to act as your bride?"

Two

At the sight of a short, curvaceous redhead being thrust into the room, Theo had started to smile. Then those tempting, full lips had parted and her words cut into him like a butcher's knife. *Hardly more than a boy!*

Eyes narrowing, he glared at her, his mood souring into a return of her critical judgement. Young, was he? Well, she was not what he'd call aged. Not the least. And she was a bit on the small side. And plump. Yes, decidedly plump, with an oddly fresh look to her for a girl from this house. Freckles dusted her nose and cheeks, as if she were a country lass, not a London harlot. But, like many a redhead, she had skin smooth as cream under the freckles.

However, he was being critical of her, he reminded himself. This whole business rode on her, after all.

Only as he tried to find fault, he found himself thinking that that pert nose of hers, and that nicely rounded chin and that oval face were all attractive enough. And she might not be too plump, for those curves kept distracting him in a way he rather liked.

Then he realized the truth.

Sallie must have coached her. Yes, that must be it. She had come in, determined to show she could be a shrew.

His shoulders eased and he offered a smile. "Lord, you could shave the hair off an ox with that sharp a tongue. But you don't have to put on any airs for this—I've no need for you to try and sound a lady."

"Airs?" she said, sounding rather affronted.

"Oh, don't you worry, Mr. Winslow," Sallie said, stepping into the room and pausing only to kick back with her foot at some bit of white cloth that now lay in the doorway. Theo could not quite see what it was, but it almost appeared to be the ties of an apron. An absurd notion that.

"Molly here can speak a proper Cockney, she can," Sallie said as she turned to the girl, and Theo could almost swear that Sallie winked at her.

Understanding appeared in the girl's eyes—wide-set, green eyes, Theo noticed, quite fetching, with a sparkle that glimmered like dew on new grass.

Turning to him, the girl said, her words only a little hesitant, "Yes, I suppose I . . . I mean, 'course I can . . . ducks."

Theo frowned at that awkward speech. Was the girl shy? Is that why she had to be pushed into the room? That wouldn't do. It'd take a girl with brass to face his father and not crumble, spilling the whole tale out as well, no doubt. That was one of the reasons he had decided he needed either an actress or the sort of woman who was hard as February ice.

Tucking his thumbs into his waistcoat pockets, he frowned and tried to put on what he hoped appeared an all-business attitude. No need to let Sallie see that his pulse—and his hopes for carrying this off—had both lifted. She'd only try to raise the rates along with it.

"Come here, then, and let's have a look at you," he said.

The girl stiffened, color pinking her cheeks under her freckles as if she was embarrassed that he wanted to inspect her. Didn't she get this every night when she paraded herself to be sold?

Sallie put a hand on the girl's back and pushed her forward. "Go on, ducks. No need to hold back as if you was waiting to hear how much he'd pay. We all know the terms, so we can all be nice and friendly."

The girl shot a rather odd look at Sallie—a look Theo could almost swear held a good deal of resistance. Had she not yet agreed to this?

"What's the problem here?" he asked, glancing at Sallie. "Is she shy?"

Sallie's smile widened, but before she could speak the girl answered. "I am not the least shy. And you do not—I mean, no need to talk about me as if I weren't here . . . ducks."

The endearment came out in a rather hostile tone and Theo glanced at her, misgivings tightening his shoulders. He rubbed the back of his neck. Perhaps he had been wrong to state his attraction to redheads—they could have the devil's temper. But she did have quite the most glorious tumble of curls. Copper highlights glinted in the red, along with golden threads and darker mahogany tones. She also had the sort of figure to draw any man's notice—round, high breasts and hips that just begged for a fellow to take hold. Not too plump in the least, really.

"I beg your pardon," he said. *And an awkward thing it is to be apologizing to a prostitute as if she were a lady.*

Then it dawned on him that her high-and-mighty attitude struck the perfect note. Yes, he needed a female who seemed to have long claws well into him, and wasn't about to let go. She had brass, right enough, and not just in the color of her hair.

Starting to smile, he came forward. "Perhaps, Sallie, you should start us off with a proper introduction?"

Sallie agreed at once. And Molly found herself unable to say much of anything as Mr. Winslow—Theodore Winslow, she learned—kept smiling at her. He had a dimple near the left corner of his mouth, and the most disarming smile. It put a mischievous gleam in his eyes, and made her want to smile back in a ridiculous, empty-headed fashion.

Then he took her hand with his ungloved one. She glanced down at his touch. Strong fingers closed over hers. Her mouth dried. Lifting her hand, he touched soft, warm lips to her skin, and then he turned her hand over and pressed a kiss into her palm. Hot pleasure washed through her.

A week with him would be no hardship. Oh, gracious, what was she thinking? Was she thinking? Why, she hardly knew him!

She wet dry lips with the tip of her tongue, then said, the words tripping out without any grace, "You still have . . . haven't answered my question. Why do you need to hire a bride?"

His smile disappeared, blue eyes darkened and she found herself facing a rather daunting gentleman. He dropped her hand. Cool air brushed her skin where a moment ago his fingers had held hers.

"Molly Sweet, eh? Well, that, my sweet Sweet, is my business. Just play your part as a vulgar sort of grasping female before my family—or at least enough so to get me disinherited—and we shall all be happy."

She blinked up at him. *Disinherited?* She had heard of odd situations that required a gentleman to marry to gain an inheritance, but she had never heard of one where a pretend bride would lose a legacy. Perhaps he was just a bit touched upstairs?

But while she did not know as much about men as did Sallie, she had spent years enough dealing with London fishmongers, grocers, and merchants that she could judge a man. And this gentleman had an honest look to him. He also had an obstinate set to his mouth, and the pulse beat rapid in a jaw clenched tight.

Stubborn as a street dog with a bone to chew, she decided.

"Very well, if that's your business, then what part is mine?" she asked.

Black eyebrows lifted with arrogant affront. "I beg your pardon?"

"Well, what am I to know about you? How did we meet? How did you come to fall in love with me—at least, I presume you did, since you proposed marriage? And why are you taking me to meet your family? Why not just run off with me? And how can I act anything if all you tell me is just to be vulgar? Oh, and grasping— just what am I to be grasping at?"

His frown tightened into a scowl. "Devil a bit, but you like questions! She always so impudent?" he asked with a glance at Sallie.

Before Sallie could say, the girl answered back. "Will you stop talking around me, as if I were not here! I am not some horse for hire. And I require at least some information before I say yes to this . . . this bargain."

"Not much of a bargain for my purse," Theo muttered. Folding his arms, he glared at the girl. Perhaps he should walk out now. Only, blazes, but she exactly suited his requirements, freckles and all. No proper lady would ever have such a common complexion. And if she could raise his hackles with just a few words, she should be able to provoke his father into one of his rages. Which is what he wanted.

The satisfaction of finally serving back his father some of his own trickled through him. Dropping his arms to his sides, he decided to humor her curiosity. He had few enough options just now, after all.

"If you must have a story, you may make up whatever you wish. Just make it believable, and I should think it obvious that what you're grasping for is a ring on your left hand. As for why I'm taking you home—oh, make something up there, too. You want to inspect your future manor, or some such thing. And for the rest, you can say the utter truth—that we met in a brothel and that I bought your time." He grinned. "My father will have an apoplexy if you do, in fact."

She stared at him, eyes widening and face paling under the freckles. "What! Do you want to kill him?"

"Of course not. Must you be so literal? I already told you I just want him to cast me off. That shouldn't be so difficult to understand? And now you can tell me if you're my girl, sweet Molly Sweet—and was there ever such a badly named female as you, for you're as tart as lemons!"

"Some consider that a fine taste. Besides, it sounds as if you want a female who'll make you trouble," Molly shot back to him, and then she remembered she really was supposed to be talking more like Sallie and not herself.

But what answer should she give him on his proposition, either in her own words, or with Sallie's odd mixture of London Cockney and artificially polished tones?

If he had seemed a libertine, if his face had shown signs of hard dissipation, or if he were not so sinfully handsome, she would have said no at once. Even for fifty pounds. But she had no sense of danger from him—and her perception for that had been well honed by the past dozen years of her life.

He could be no more than in his midtwenties, she guessed, and he sounded honestly desperate to be rid of this inheritance. She could not imagine why. She had never been willed more than her mother's locket and her father's sword—both now long gone, taken from her when she'd been found on her own at the London docks and sent to St. Marylebone. But how lovely to have someone care enough to bequeath something to one—only he seemed not to think so.

So did she help him or not?

And did she help herself to fifty pounds?

But when she took a breath and looked at the situation, the blunt truth was that she wanted to go with him. The money just made it all the more tempting.

It surprised her, this sudden fierce ache. This longing. Shocked her to her core. But she could not deny that he had a face and form made to put ideas in any female mind—and it made her look to her future and wonder if she would ever have such a chance as this again. A fine gentleman of her own. Even if only pretend. Even if only for a week.

Well, she had to be honest about it. She wanted to pretend with him.

Even if it did not last.

What, after all, did—good or bad?

Brushing her fingers along her hand where his lips had touched her skin, her face warm, she glanced from him to Sallie.

Why not agree? Sallie thought it easy money. And he might kiss her hand again. Of course he might try to kiss a few other parts of her, as well.

Sallie gave an encouraging nod and lifted her eyebrows as if to urge her agreement. And with that, Molly made up her mind. It would not be the biggest risk she had ever taken, but it did rank high.

Still, she had taken a risk to come home to England after Uncle Fred died. She had taken a greater risk to hire on with Sallie and escape a return to St. Marylebone, with its overcrowded rooms and its stench of poverty and hopelessness. And if this adventure only led to a week with him, well, she could think of worse things.

The trick would be to make certain this did not become one of those worse things.

Squaring her shoulders, she stretched as tall as she could. "If I have your word as a gentleman that you'll never do more than I allow, then I shall . . . that's to say, I'm you're girl, ducks."

The blue eyes blazed again. "Word as a . . . ? Never do . . . ? Just who is footing the bill, here, my girl?"

"Now, now, Mr. Winslow," Sallie said, smoothly inserting herself and laying a hand on his arm. "We agreed on terms, and they're quite generous, given as you're not paying near to a full night's rate for Molly's time."

Not near to a full night's rate? Theo glanced at the redhead, impressed and rather curious now. There must be something quite extraordinary under that dress of hers to command more than a hundred and fifty for a full night. Blazes, but what talents did she have?

Sallie leaned closer to him, her voice low and teasing his imagination. "Where else, I ask you, will you find just what you asked for?"

He frowned. She was all a fellow could ask for. Sharp tongue and all. And to have her for a week—well, perhaps this was a standard ploy to squeak a few more quid from him. With a week's time, he might well find a way to soften that tongue of hers and her mercenary attitude. He'd coaxed more than a few ladies into changing their minds about what they'd offer.

"Very well, Miss Sweet, you have my word as a gentleman that I won't do more than you allow. But in turn I want a guarantee. If I'm not disowned, then I owe you nothing!"

Sallie put a hand on her hip. "You don't want much do you now! Molly's time for free if you don't get your way."

"You said you liked your gentlemen to go away satisfied. Well, that's what I'm asking for." He raked his glance over the girl again. "Or don't you think you'll be able to carry this off?"

The girl stretched taller, though her head still only came to his shoulder—and it would rest nicely there, too, he thought.

"Twenty-five pounds for my time, no matter the outcome. And the balance then if you are disowned."

"Ten," he countered.

"Twenty."

"Done." He grinned at her. "Do we seal our bargain with a kiss?"

Dark-reddish eyebrows lifted. "At those rates? I think not. But here's my hand on it."

He took her hand, noticing that traces of white powder dusted her skin—trying to hide her freckles, he wondered? Lifting her hand, he flecked his tongue across her skin. Flour, of all things! Must be some new beauty secret.

And then he forgot about it for she flushed deliciously, pinking up like a maid of May, in fact.

Pulling her hand away, her eyes glittered and her lips parted as if she looked ready to offer back another of her saucy answers, but Sallie caught her arm.

Leading her from her room, Sallie called back, "I'll just see she's packed and ready within the hour."

"Quarter hour, mind. It's a warm day and I've left Terrance's team being walked long enough as it is."

"Hour? Quarter hour? But what about my tarts?"

Theo frowned at such an obscure comment from the girl. But Sallie merely waved it aside, promised she'd see to all, then she had Molly out the door and the door closed behind them.

Molly turned to her, already shaking her head. "I cannot possibly leave today. There are instructions about the kitchen—Edna shall have to manage it while I'm away."

"Ducks, if Edna can't run that kitchen after being with you for near on two years now, she's a half-wit, and I don't think she'd fancy you callin' her that to her face. Why she's probably already got your pastries done and finished."

"But . . . but I have menus made up only until Saturday."

Sallie linked her arm with Molly's as she started up the stairs to the girls' rooms. "Send me more in the post—or, better yet, Edna can use some from last month. It's the food that goes off, not the bits of paper you write it all down on."

"But I . . ." *I have no more excuses,* Molly thought, panic spiraling loose. She thought of the gentleman, with his skin-tight buckskins and his beautiful blue coat, and his silk-embroidered yellow waistcoat so casually worn. Then she found one more. "I have nothing to wear that looks as if I am a . . . a hired woman."

Oh, gracious, what have I just leapt into?

Sallie gave a scornful glance at Molly's dress. "Ducks, you haven't enough gowns to look even half proper, let alone improper. We'll have to see what Jane left. She took her best with her, but she spent what she made on her back putting cloth on it, so there ought to be something. A few stitches to take up the hems and they'll do. Now stop havering. You said you'd do it, so stop thinking why you can't. Just think of the money, ducks. It's what gets me through anything."

"The money," Molly repeated, pressing a hand to her stomach. It was just that those blue eyes no longer dazzled and that handsome face no longer overwhelmed—how did a man ever get such beauty? Such hard, masculine beauty. Even features and a firm chin and a straight nose ought not to have such an effect. But they did. As had those dark eyebrows set low over his eyes, which flattened and quirked and lifted to display his every mood.

She could think again without those broad shoulders looming before her. Without him in the room, restless and somehow drawing all attention. And the images dancing through her mind were all disaster—she was about to go off with some gentleman she did not even know.

Of course, she had done almost the same when she had met Sallie—and that had turned out well enough.

Still, she had learned enough about caution, so she turned to Sallie, desperate for advice. "What am I to do if he doesn't honor his word—if he wants, well, if he tries to make me act like one of your girls?"

"That's easy, ducks. Smile, put a hand on your hip, and name a price that'll take the interest right out of him."

Molly thought about that. And she thought of those intense, direct eyes of his and the impression she had of focused concentration. "I could name five hundred pounds and he still might say he would pay."

"Oh, he might say it, but you just ask for coins in your open hand before anything else opens wide, and see if that don't act like a dash of cold water."

"That actually sounds like Mr. Tipton's usual attitude," she said. Sallie turned a questioning stare on her, so she added, "He's the fishmonger who comes on Thursdays."

"Well, you want to make sure you ain't a trout with your mouth gapping open to be hooked by this flash gent, or any other. Remember that, or you'll be agreeing to more than you think you will now. And just you remember, too, every woman may have her price, but every man has his limits. Most of 'em start with his purse. Now, let's see how those dresses look. You're going to have to be dazzlin', 'cause it's going to take us longer than a quarter hour to turn you out in style."

By the time Sallie finished, Molly no longer recognized herself. Nell and Harriet, seeing the door open to Jane's forsaken room, had poked their heads in—eyes sleepy and hair tumbled and still in their night wrappers. Sallie's house kept late hours and late mornings. Sallie bustled them out, saying to Molly afterwards, "Never does to stir up jealousy, and you don't want them thinking you're stealing their trade."

"Gracious, I suppose I am. Do you think they'll be angry with me?"

"Not if you don't go talking about the money. Always

brings out the worst in folks, if you do. And don't you let that gent of yours start talking price with you, either. You don't want him thinking he can argue you down. That's why the girls always leave it to me to set the rates."

Molly paused in smoothing a hand over a rather pretty scarlet jacket that Jane had left behind. "I almost forgot— what should I give you of the fifty pounds as your share?"

Sallie abruptly buried herself in Jane's half-empty wardrobe. "Lord, the girl had more clothes than in a Drury Lane play, no wonder she couldn't pack them all. And don't you worry over my share. I took my percentage off the top as usual, so that fifty pounds is yours right and proper." Emerging from the wardrobe with a peacock-blue silk gown in a paisley pattern, she held it up. "Now see if this'll fit, and then we've got to get a trunk packed."

The dress did fit—or near enough. It laced up the back, and had to be tied loose, for Jane was slimmer. "I'm almost spilling out the top," Molly protested as she looked at herself.

"That's the point. Hold still while I pin it. You'll have to hem it later. I'll have Nipton pack you a sewing kit," Sallie said, speaking of her own maid.

With that, she sent Molly off to her room to change into a striped walking dress and to finish her packing.

Ten minutes later, Sallie reappeared, smiling like a cat with a full belly and feathers scattered around her, and with her hand over the shift-pocket sewn into her underdress.

Uneasy with what that secret smile might mean, Molly asked, "You seem pleased about something?"

"Oh, just settled a few things with Mr. Winslow. I think you'll find him right easy to deal with. Always such a pleasure to find a flash cove who knows how to act a gent. Now, mind you, no talking money with him! And don't you look just grand in that dress!"

Molly glanced down at herself. The striped walking

dress, in lime green and canary yellow, was cut narrow, the muslin so fine that it brushed her skin, soft as cream. Over it she wore a solid green Spencer, the short jacket cut so close that Molly felt almost like meat stuffed into a sausage skin.

"Just one thing you need, ducks. Hold on a tick."

Sallie hurried from the room, coming back a few minutes later with a straw bonnet. An extravagant brim rose up, trimmed with two green ostrich feathers and artificial cherries.

Settling the bonnet in place, Sallie tied the yellow silk grosgrain ribbons under Molly's chin. "There, that's the prize. Now, let's show you off to your gent."

"My gent," Molly repeated, a tickle of pleasure and uncertainty dancing through her.

She had on her own gloves and boots, but nothing else was hers. Not even the silk stockings, found at the back of Jane's wardrobe. "I can do this," she muttered. "For fifty pounds, I can do this."

Sallie followed her down the stairs. "Low, grasping, vulgar—that's what he wants. You can be as bold as those stripes you're wearing."

"Bold," Molly echoed. How in heavens did Sallie's girls go through this night after night, going off with gentlemen they hardly knew? She had often wondered, and had been a little envious, for some of the girls had told her that she had no idea of the pleasure she was missing. Now, however, she began to wonder if the girls had left out any mention of the anxiety of such casual meetings. Or perhaps they did not notice.

Still, she'd done well with her bargain. He had agreed to her terms, and she had Sallie's advice to help keep him to his promise. And he looked gentleman enough that he would keep his word—besides, there was something he wanted from her, other than her person. He wanted his disinheritance, and for that he needed her cooperation. That alone reassured her that he would keep his part of this arrangement.

With such thoughts tumbling through her, and with her breath short and her nerves taut, she came to the top of the stairs, looked down into the hall where Mr. Winslow waited, his tall beaver hat in his hands, and she smiled.

Then he glanced up, his expression set tight and those blue eyes flashing, and Molly wanted to turn around and go back to her kitchen.

Three

Theo glanced up, his attention drawn by the squeak of a stair and his temper worn with waiting. A quarter hour he had said—that had been at least three-quarters of an hour ago! He parted his lips to issue a rebuke, and then he saw her and a pleasurable shock scorched through him.

Gone was the plain white gown, replaced by something in bright stripes. The fabric clung to her hips and hinted at the soft narrowing of her waist before disappearing under a short, dark jacket that fit as near to a second skin as any man could wish over ample, high breasts.

Lord, but she looked about as far from respectable as a woman could get. He smiled.

Then he glanced up at her face and saw what looked like apprehension in those wide, green eyes.

Ah, knows she kept me waiting, and she's sorry for it, he thought, in a mood now to be pleased.

"Blazes, but my father will throw us both out of the house with you done up like that!"

She seemed to grip the newel post even tighter as she frowned and asked, "Is something wrong? I thought the dress quite—quite attractive?"

He grinned. "It's more than that. Now, come along. Your carriage awaits, my sweet Sweet. However did you come up with such a name?"

"By being born with it," she said, her tone sharpening.

She started down the stairs, and he watched, his attention caught by the sway of hips and the hint of trim ankle he glimpsed as she lifted her skirts for each step.

Two steps above him, she stopped, dropped her skirts and then gave him her gloved hand. "I am putting myself in your care, Mr. Winslow."

The gesture and the words carried an odd grace, as if she honestly meant them. A swell of protective instinct rose. Short, petite fingers lay in his grip, slim and fragile as fine china. He frowned. Quite ridiculous, of course. A jade such as her must care only for the size of a fellow's purse. This would be no more than a trick of her trade to stir a fellow's interest.

Blazes, she was good at it, too.

Still, they had a game to play now. So he tucked her hand into the crook of his elbow. Might as well start treating her as if she honestly were his intended—it'd take a bit to get accustomed to the thought of having a female attached to him.

And he fought down the shiver of apprehension. Hadn't Terrance always warned him against too much of an attachment to any female? 'Course, it would have been a fine thing for him to have heeded his own advice, but Terrance never did. So it was now up to him to pull his brother's irons out of this particular fire.

With a tip of his hat to Sallie—who had his fifty pounds in her clutches now—Theo settled his high-crown beaver at a jaunty angle. Then he said to Molly, "Hope you don't mind traveling in an open carriage."

The page boy leapt up from his chair to open the front door for them, and Theo led his vulgarly dressed pretend bride from Sallie's house.

Soon as he got her to the front steps she stopped, and he glanced down. Her eyes had brightened and widened. "Gracious, that's your carriage?"

He glanced at the curricle, and almost wished it were.

Black, with touches of red trim and red painted wheels, it looked sleek and expensive; Terrance had always preferred how the light-bodied curricle handled on the road to the precarious perch of the high phaeton. Burke, Terrance's groom, short and slight, his face weathered by the sun and dressed in black coat and trousers, his hat at a rakish angle in imitation of how Terrance wore his, stood beside the heads of a pair of bay horses.

The sun pulled flashes of red from the fit, brown bodies of the compact pair of horses. Black tails were banged flat, the hair trimmed just below the hocks, and black manes lay to the left in perfect order. About the only thing in his brother's life that ran smoothly was his stable, Theo thought, a touch of pride stirring. Of course, a fellow ought to have a well run stable.

"My brother's curricle," he explained. Then, unable to resist boasting, he added, "The suspension is quite the latest—S-springs, don't you know. And you won't see a pair as well matched as these. They're Terrance's, too. I figured he owed me at least their loan, for they've bottom enough to handle the drive to Somerset if you don't try to gallop the whole distance."

"Now, come along and up with you. You'll sit next to me, and I've a rug, if you wish. It may be warm now, but we'll pick up a breeze on the road."

Fitting his hands to her waist, he found that she indeed had a figure just made for a fellow to hold. Soft as sin in all the right spots. He let his hands stay longer than he needed to before he lifted her into the front seat above the large carriage wheels. She seemed not to notice his touch and he found that a little irritating. Of course she must be well used to being handled by gentlemen, but he still found himself wanting her to be more aware of him.

Oh, stuff it. She's a hired woman!

Stepping up into the carriage, he picked up the reins and called out to the groom, "Let 'em go, Burke."

The groom stepped away from the tossing heads of the bays. They started forward, the white of their legs flashing. Over-grained and under used, Theo had always thought. He had been glad of finding them tucked in the mews behind the house that his brother kept in London. And the surly Burke, too, who'd helped the horses into harness after a suitable bribe had softened his stance against Theo borrowing so much as a leather strap.

As the carriage swept away from Sallie's house, Burke swung himself up and into the small seat behind Theo and Molly, then he leaned forward and said, his tone impertinent and rough with a West Country accent, "Now you mind, don't you go tippin' us over!"

Theo glanced back at him. "Tip us—? Just you hold your tongue, or I'll set you down again."

"Ha. See if you can! I'm going where those bays go."

"Then stubble it. Terrance may pay you, but the day I can't handle the ribbons better than he ever did is the day I take up driving cart horses. Tip us over!"

He glanced at Molly Sweet who stared at him, wide-eyed and looking a touch alarmed. Her hand gripped the edge of the black coach hood that had been folded back and which could be lifted over them in case of bad weather.

"I've never tipped over any carriage," he told her, then had to admit, "Well, other than that first cart, and it wasn't my fault for that blasted pony ran off with it. So settle back and enjoy yourself, my sweet Sweet, and we'll be to Winslow Park in no time."

She offered a weak smile, then turned her face forward. But, he noted with a touch of irritation, she did not let go her hold on the edge of the carriage hood.

So much for thinking her to be what she looked— a sweet, trusting soul.

* * *

Two hours later, Molly sat on the green verge beside a hard, dusty road. The leaves of an oak shaded her as she watched Theo—they had progressed to first names within a half hour, when passing through Hounslow. She had been delighted to see London streets and houses give way to countryside. They had attracted a few stares while in town—no doubt due to the smart carriage—but in leaving the city they also left behind the street gawkers and other carriages. So far only the mail coach for Bath had passed them on the road.

True to his claim, Theo did drive well. At least she thought he did. He set the pair of bays to a steady trot, easing them back when they tried to break into a canter to follow the galloping mail coach, and smoothly guiding the pair as if the reins were extensions of his arms.

With white clouds dotting the blue sky, drifting idly, rather like fat, lazy sheep, and the weather fair, Molly had begun to relax and enjoy herself.

Her companion had not much to say for himself. He stared ahead, jaw set, eyes dark, as if brooding about something—that bone of his, she thought. Or perhaps the groom's insults to his skills. Shrugging off his mood, she had sat back against the well padded leather cushions—the carriage rocking from the horse's brisk trot, the breeze cool on her face, ruffling the ostrich feathers against her cheek—and had given herself to the parade of aromas.

Smells of the city—horse dung, chamber pots emptied into the streets, coal fires—gave way to cut hay, cow pastures, and teasing wisps of flowery scents that she could not identify. It was new enough that she did not even mind the dust, dry as the road was from summer and a day without rain. She had been to India and back as a child, but since her return to London, she had never been farther than an excursion to Richmond Park. Vague memories of her earliest years stirred, memories of green countryside—but they slipped away.

Then, on an open stretch between any village or town, one of the horses started to bob its head. Cursing under his breath, Theo had pulled the carriage to a halt, easing it off the road and onto the grassy verge. After jumping down from the carriage, he strode to the horses' heads, the groom already there ahead of him to hold the animals.

The two had set to arguing, blame and curses flying like smoke from cooking oil spilled onto a fire.

Molly had waited for a few moments, then had grown bored and stiff. Climbing down from the carriage, she glanced around her. The gentlemen, bent over as they were to stare at the horse's leg, had seemed not to notice and that suited her.

She had walked a bit, and found it too warm to do more, and so she had found her seat under the oak tree. And still Theo and his groom, Burke, stared at one of the horse's front legs, lifting it, then putting it down, feeling down the back of it, all the time conferring in low voices, both of them frowning and looking a little guilty.

In the warmth of the sun-dappled shade, Molly's eyes began to drift closed.

"Well, he's lame!"

Eyes startled opening, Molly straightened. Theo's voice sounded tense with anger.

Arms folded, he stood next to her, glaring at the carriage where Burke had begun to unbuckle harness straps, his face set into deep, frowning lines. "Thrown a shoe, and gotten himself a stone bruise by the looks of it. Blazes, but these roads are hard as iron! I'm going to have to send Burke back to Twyford for a fresh pair."

"Won't a new shoe help?"

He glanced at her. "Did you not hear me say he'd bruised his frog with a stone?"

"Frog? I thought he was a horse?"

Theo rolled his eyes and began to drag off his driving gloves. "The frog is the soft part of a horse's hoof—could you walk after pounding your foot on a rock if all I did was to put new shoes on you? You dashed well could not. No, he'll need a few days rest. Burke will have to walk them back, and there's no telling how long it will take him to bring a fresh pair."

"Can he not ride the one horse and lead the other?"

He shot her a scornful glance, then said, his tone dry, "These are carriage horses."

"Oh," she said, nodding as if this made any sense to her. The horses she recalled from her childhood in India had been trained for both riding and driving, but perhaps that was because they had all been military horses. She also had distant memories of her father taking her up before him, and her mother had ridden. But London had held no opportunity to renew any acquaintance with anything equine. One had to be rich to afford a horse.

Glancing up at Theo, she studied his scowling face. "It could be worse." He turned to her, so she offered a smile. "It could be raining."

With a sigh, he threw himself onto the grass next to her, careless of how it might stain his coat or his buff buckskin breeches. "Or it could have been a ligament— Terrance would skin me for that. Still, it's damned nuisance. I'd hoped to make Hungerford today—and there's the cost of sound horses to be had now. I hadn't expected that. Well, I shall just have to hope I can fetch the bays back sound again before Terrance finds out."

"Would he really—skin you?"

Propping himself on his elbow, Theo took off his hat. He dragged his hand through his hair, disordering it utterly so that one black lock fell over his lined forehead. "Blister me at the least."

"Really? How awful!"

Theo lifted one shoulder in a shrug. "Oh, he's a capital fellow really—quite the best of brothers. But he does have a temper worse than your own."

"I do not—that is, I don't have no temper, ducks. Least not much of one."

"Oh yes you do. Hold on a bit. Burke has them unharnessed and I'd best give him enough blunt to get a decent pair. Lord knows what we'll get, but if they're too dreadful, I can change 'em when they're blown."

He rose.

Molly watched, admiring the loose, easy grace with which he moved. A breeze ruffled his hair like a lover's hand.

She glanced down at the hat and gloves he had left beside her. He did not wear cologne, she noted. Pulling off her own gloves, she smoothed a finger across the fine nap of the beaver-skin. He seemed a gentleman who disliked encumbrances. Was that why he wished to be rid of his inheritance?

He finished giving money and instructions to the sour-faced Burke, who grumbled words of doom for both of them when Terrance learned of this, and then Burke started walking back along the road, the horses led behind him.

"Poor Burke," Molly said, as Theo stretched out in the grassy shade beside her.

"Poor what?"

"Well, to have to walk miles in the heat and dust. And he seems so unhappy about this."

He offered up a sudden grin, which crooked his mouth. "I have never seen a day when 'poor Burke' hasn't been anything but the worst doomsayer in England. You'd think he'd be happy working in a stable that boasts the kind of horseflesh as my brother owns. But don't you go pitying him. He's well paid, and he'll get to Twyford and demand the best ale for himself and their best care for his master's horse. And he'll get them, too."

"You sound rather fond of him."

"Oh, Burke's a good enough sort. Once you get past the sour side of him. Taught me how to ride, in fact."

"What? He hardly looks old enough to be shaving!"

"That's his size. I've a suspicion he had ambitions once to ride as a jockey—he certainly did for my father for a time."

"And why did he not continue? Did something happen?"

He glanced at her, eyes puzzled and black eyebrows lowered flat. "My sweet, Sweet, I don't go inquiring into the personal lives of my father's servants. It would be damned prying and rude of me!"

"As I'm being now?" She turned away. Propping up her feet, she folded her hands on her knees.

"Taken a pet now?" he asked, his voice coaxing.

She wouldn't look at him. "No, I have not."

"Oh, come along. We've hours to pass, and I don't fancy spending them staring at sheep and grass."

Glancing at him from the corner of her eyes, she asked, "Does that mean I may ask prying, rude questions then?" She added a belated, "Ducks?"

"I suppose it does," he said, his eyes lightening with humor. "Though it doesn't mean I'll answer them."

"Then I'd rather talk about myself. Did you know that I once lived in India? I am rather proud of that, for I think it gives me a touch of the exotic. Don't you, ducks?"

"No. But you must have looked exotic there—that red hair and pale skin among the Hindus."

"Not all the natives are Hindu—but they are all rather remarkable people. I rather miss them. And the food. Oh, the spices are heaven. And the land is one of the most extraordinary contrasts of beauty and harsh ugliness. But I don't miss the heat. Not at all. But what about you? Have you traveled?"

He stood and stripped off his coat, which he then tossed to the ground beside his hat before stretching out again. He looked even better, she thought, sneaking an admiring glance, without his coat on. The white sleeves of his shirt billowed loose, and his waistcoat hugged his lean, muscular body.

Propping himself on one elbow, he plucked a blade of grass and began to chew on the pale end of it. "Not particularly. Though it's my plan to do so after my father disowns me."

"Won't that upset your mother—and your brother?"

He gave a short, harsh laugh. "I don't see Terrance being upset in the least about anything. And my mother's dead."

She nodded, then said, her tone matter of fact, "Mine is too."

Theo lay still for a moment, surprised. He had expected, and braced himself for, the usual artificial sympathy, the sort that generally masked the unspoken relief that tragedy had struck elsewhere. Now he realized how harshly he had spoken, in anticipation of any pity from her.

She seemed not even to notice, however, for she just sat there with her knees pulled up close to her, looking more like a girl than a woman of ill-repute.

Lifting her head, she undid the ribbons of her bonnet, and he smiled as she took it off. What a pleasure she was to look at, with that glorious hair and those enticing curves. No wonder she cost what she did for a night. And he had her for far more than that—'course, it was all supposed to be look and no touch, but he had not yet tried to persuade her into just a bit more.

"I was—what, ten—no, I was nine when she died," she

said, eyes distant. "Cholera. Everyone dreaded it. At least the Europeans and English did. The natives had a rather fatalistic view—karma—fate—they called it, I think." She turned to him. "What about you? How old were you?"

He lifted a shoulder and looked away, not wanting to touch those memories. "I hardly remember."

She made an understanding sound and he glanced at her again. She had her cheek resting on her hand and her head turned towards him, and she looked adorable.

"What do you think is better—to have lots of memories?" she said, rocking herself gently. "Or to lose a parent before it really matters? I had a younger brother, but he died on the voyage to India. I only know about him because my mother once showed me a locket with a snippet of his hair. And I could only feel guilty, for I honestly could not work up even a single tear over him."

He sat up and leaned closer. "That's it exactly. I can only remember my father making everyone dress in black, and no one allowed to do anything. No running, no playing. I used to escape to the woods just so they wouldn't see me enjoying myself while everyone else went around with faces like black clouds."

"It's difficult, isn't it? My uncle used to say that tears are only about feeling sorry for yourself, for if you believe in a heaven, you ought to be happy for anyone who's gone there. He used to say he liked to think of them as having gone off to Brighton for holiday."

Theo gave a snort. "Brighton? Not exactly my idea of heaven. But who do you mean by them?"

"Why my father and mother, of course. I lost them both—such an odd way of putting it, as if I mislaid them, but it sounds so harsh to just say they died."

He stared at her. She had not a trace of self-pity in her eyes or expression, but gazed back at him, a slight smile lifting her lips, her eyes bright.

"You are an extraordinary woman," he said, his voice

soft. Her laugh bubbled loose, giggly as a girl's. He couldn't help but grin back. "What? What is so funny about that?"

"I'm as ordinary as you can find—other than for my hair. Plain Molly Sweet, a bit of a girl with no family and not much else going for her other than God's grace. And there are times I wish that stretched just a bit further than it has for a common girl like me."

He sat up. "Now who filled your head with such nonsense? Common! Does Sallie tell you that?"

"Oh, no, Sallie's been one of the better blessings. But the workhouse. . . ." Even in the warmth of the day, she shuddered.

He knew little enough about such places, other than that they were established to help the poor—give them shelter at the least, and perhaps opportunities to find a position if someone came to them. Frowning, he asked, "I thought they're supposed to take care of you in such a place?"

With a shake of her head, she looked away. "I don't want to speak of it." Then she looked back, smiling, her accent roughening again. "Let's talk of good memories, ducks. Why don't you tell me about your brother?"

And so he did, happy to amuse her.

He told the story of how he had once followed Terrance, thinking to discover his brother's favorite fishing spot but had instead found his brother intimately entangled with a neighbor's wife. And how Terrance had first brought him to London and shown him the gaming hells to avoid and the brothels to frequent. And how Terrance and he had once held up the mail coach. "We actually didn't steal anything—we only wanted to see if anyone would actually 'stand or deliver' but Terrance's horse kept wanting to bolt with him every time he started to shout and I just about fell off my own horse laughing."

She had laughed at that herself, and he decided he

could not have asked for a better audience. At the more outrageous stories—such as the time Terrance was caught at a ball in an indiscreet position with not one, but two ladies, both of them older than himself—her cheeks pinked. And he found himself wondering how she had managed, at Sallie's house, to keep such an ability.

He also found himself telling more and more of the disreputable stories, just to see her mouth pucker with prim disapproval, as if she had no such similar stories in her own past.

With a rueful laugh, Molly shook her head. "Your brother sounds an incorrigible knave—and you sound proud that he is."

"Incorrigible? Now that's a fine word, coming from you."

"I'll have you know—" Molly broke off her protest, realizing she had been about to proclaim her virtue. Face warm, she lifted one shoulder. "Some of us are bad because we don't have much choice in it."

And she would have added more disapproval of his brother, except that she had heard the pride in his voice. Even during the worst stories, it had been there—a thread of admiration for his brother's daring, his lack of concern for what others thought, his growing notoriety.

In truth, his brother sounded a disaster. But to say that to Theo seemed as if it would only be courting an argument.

As she thought on it, she realized a pang of envy lay under her faultfinding.

How lovely to have someone to care about. To have close family and ties.

She straightened. Might as well wish to have wings. She really had to keep in mind that she had come with this handsome fellow for his fifty pounds.

Only it was rather difficult with him gazing at her, a bemused smile lifting the corner of his mouth, his eyes sparkling with some mischief.

"Penny for your thoughts, ducks," she asked, curious now just what did stir that light in his eyes.

His smile widened and then he said, "I'm thinking about how much I want to kiss you."

Four

Molly stared at him. Her pulse beat faster in her throat. The drone of a bee hummed past her ear. The breeze, soft and light, touched her cheek, and it lifted the lock of black hair that lay across his forehead. His eyes had gone dark, as deep and vivid a blue as the open sea.

If she sat still, he would kiss her. She knew it. Knew it in her muscles and bones and in the blood that sang through her—with fear or anticipation?

Mouth parched, she could think of no answer to give him. No quip such as Sallie might have to turn away desire. And no reason for her own mad curiosity as to what his lips might feel like on hers.

Utter, utter madness.

He would know in an instant that she lacked any skill. She might be only a cook in a house of ill-repute, but she had overheard and had seen what went on—a good deal of it carried out not behind closed doors but in hallways and in Sallie's parlor and even once she had glimpsed them on the stairs. And she had never been kissed—never could kiss anyone—like one of Sallie's girls.

Or could she?

He leaned closer, his movement slow, almost as if he, too, drifted nearer on the breeze. The smile on his lips faded and a curious intensity lit his eyes.

Why must he be so handsome? she thought, her pulse hammering faster now. The faintest shading of beard darkened his jaw. She noted the twin furrows that lined his forehead. *He worries too much over something,* she thought. And she wanted to smooth those grooves with her fingers.

But she held still. Afraid to move. Afraid to betray herself. Afraid that he would soon know she wasn't the loose woman he thought her.

And since she did not know what else to do, she fastened her stare on his mouth—a beautiful mouth, lower lip full, top lips curving at the center and thinning at the ends. His lips parted, and hers copied them. Then she drew a deep, ragged breath and held it.

I can't do this!

Only she would.

His mouth hovered over hers, nearly touching, his breath mixing with hers in a hot caress.

A shout and the beat of hooves startled them both. Theo jerked upright and away from her.

She turned as well, letting out the breath she had been holding with a giddy sense of relief edged by irritated disappointment. Perhaps God looked after her better than even she knew. But it would have been nice if that shout had come just a few moments later.

A wicked thought, indeed. She really would have to mind these wayward inclinations that this fellow stirred in her, or she might well end up one of Sallie's girls. *Remember your fifty pounds and your inn,* she told herself sternly.

Taking up her bonnet, she rose, saying brightly, "Burke is back."

"So he is," Theo grumbled, pushing himself to his feet.

The groom rode in a gig, next to what looked a gentleman farmer with his loose-fitting brown coat, his black top-boots and buff breeches and his black slouch hat. Two horses trotted behind the two-wheeled carriage, led by long lines that Burke held.

Theo reached down to retrieve his coat, hat, and gloves, and then he let out a frustrated breath as he glanced at his sweet Molly Sweet. Such a near thing, that kiss. Temptingly near. Well, at least she hadn't pushed him away with a reminder of her price. He would take that as a good sign.

She had tied that ridiculous bonnet of hers back onto her head, leaving the feathers to tickle her cheek. Lord, she was a saucy piece—slipping into that polished accent of hers as if she were out to impress him. Or perhaps it was habit with her, to act the lady for a better price.

Well, no matter. As long as she sounded appallingly low in front of his father that would do nicely. In the meantime, he had a night on the road with her to look forward to, and another day's travel before they reached Somerset.

And if he couldn't get at least a kiss from her in that time then he wasn't Terrance Winslow's brother.

With his mood properly cheered by that thought, he went forward to greet the gentleman farmer whose horses he seemed to be hiring.

Burke had the horses—not a bad pair, Theo thought, running a critical eye over them, mismatched in color as they were—in harness long before the gentleman farmer had finished a long-winded introduction of himself. He kept grinning at Molly and hinting of her happiness, and Theo realized that Burke must have said something about her being a bride.

Offering a grin, Theo used the excuse to slip an arm around her waist. The gentleman farmer gave an indulgent smile, wished them happy again, and soon enough they were on the road again.

The hired pair went well, though the gray gelding tended to fall back, as if lazy and trying to leave the work to the brown mare next to him. They reached Reading easily enough that day and stopped for refreshments, which they took outside The Crown, under an apple tree.

"Best eat your fill," Theo advised Molly, settling himself on the bench next to her, a mug of ale in hand. "We won't stop for dinner until after the light is gone."

Molly glanced down at the cold meat pie that a maid from the tavern had brought her. She picked at the heavy, sodden crust and wrinkled her nose. It took a light hand to make a light pastry—and that set her to wondering if Edna had gotten the tarts in? And had she burnt the edges again with too hot a fire? Edna still tended to get frazzled when trying to juggle the preparation of more than half a dozen dishes at the same time, and now Molly found time to worry over her kitchen.

Only it wasn't hers really. It was Sallie's. And she was here working for a kitchen that really would be her own.

After pushing away the pie, she picked up her cup of tea from the plank table that had been set under the tree for guests of the inn. "Thank you . . . I mean, thanks, ducks, but I'm not at all hungry."

He gave a shrug, told her to suit herself. And when she finished her tea and the horses had rested an hour they set out again.

Daylight held until well past nine, when the sky began to darken into purple. Molly had been swaying in her seat for the past half hour by then. Her eyes kept sliding shut and twice she had had to jerk herself upright to keep from either falling out of the open curricle or leaning against Theo. She felt hollowed out, though it wasn't food she wanted but a bed—a nice, unmoving, soft bed.

When the lights of a town glimmered ahead of them, showing through the trees, she straightened, hope trickling into her that they would stop at last. The last time she had traveled so far had been that endless ship voyage home from India.

"Hungerford," Theo said, his teeth flashing white against the gathering twilight. How he saw to guide the horses she didn't know. To her, the road looked as dark as the fields to either side. "Not quite the hour I expected to reach it, but The Three Swans should do for us. It's a good sight better than stopping at The Pelican back in Speenhamland—there's a reason its sign shows a bird with a long bill."

Molly offered up a weak smile at this play on words for the inn's name and supposed cost, and then she smothered a yawn with her hand. And her eyelids drifted lower.

Then, suddenly, the curricle stopped moving.

Blinking, she sat up. She must have nodded off for as she looked around now she could not remember seeing any of the town, nor did she recall Theo's turning into the inn's yard. Yet the carriage stood still—blessedly so—with Burke already at the horses' heads. She glanced around, relieved, every muscle aching, and already picturing the welcoming softness of a bed. Any bed.

Two stable boys had emerged with lanterns carried high and she could just make out the two-story structure of the inn. Brick, she thought, with a gabled roof, though her eyes did not seem to want to focus on more than that.

"Come along," Theo said, his voice brisk as ever. Where ever did he come by so much energy? She glanced down to see him waiting, his hand stretched up to help her down. Once on the ground she leaned against him, grateful for the support of hard muscle and his tall frame.

His voice softened. "You look done in."

Looking up at him, she offered a smile. "Who'd have thought that sitting all day could be so wearing?"

"Yes, well, a wash and a meal and you'll be right as ninepins," he said, leading her inside the inn.

They paused in the hallway and Molly squinted against the brightness of oil lamps and candlelight. The rumble of male voices carried from the public room that lay to the right of them, mixing with a fiddle's bright melody. Aromas of roast meat and baking bread drifted from the kitchen, which seemed to be tucked behind the stairs, and Molly's stomach rumbled. Well, perhaps she did want just a little to eat before she slept.

As they waited, a lady in a brown traveling dress started down the stairs. Molly glanced up at her, offering a slight smile. The lady at once stopped her descent. Her glance swept over Molly, far more chill than the summer night air, then she turned around and hurried up the stairs again.

Molly frowned at such poor manners. Had the lady forgotten something? But before her tired mind could weave an answer to such a rude about-face, a stout fellow came forward from the back of the inn. He wore an apron over his breeches—the innkeep, Molly decided, and her hopes for a bed began to fade as he looked them over, his mouth pulling down and even more disdain in his eyes than had been in the glance of the lady on the stair.

His tone wary and rough, he asked, "And what might I do for you?"

Theo had already taken off his hat and now he pulled off his driving gloves as he said, his tone indifferent, as if he had not even noticed the disapproval being directed at them, "We need a meal and a set of rooms for the night."

The innkeeper's stare raked her over again and Molly saw herself for the first time as others must. Gracious, but she ought to have expected this. But she had been so long at Sallie's house she had not realized that she now looked exactly what she was pretending to be, what she was, in fact—a bought woman.

Now she compared the lady's brown traveling dress, with its high neck and elegant lines, to her own gown, with its tight jacket, too-bright colors, and clinging skirts. So that was what Theo had actually meant when he said she looked more than attractive. Of course he would think so.

The innkeeper's nose went up and he fixed a cold stare on Theo. "This is a respectable inn. You can take a meal in the tap room, but then you take your fancy piece elsewhere!"

Theo stiffened and Molly glanced at him, apprehensive. The easy-going young gentleman of a moment ago had disappeared into blazing blue eyes that narrowed dangerously and a face that had unexpectedly hardened. "My fancy . . . what the blazes do you mean insulting me? And my wife!"

Molly's face chilled. She tugged on Theo's arm. "Please do not make a scene on my behalf."

The pulse beat hard and strong in his jaw, and his eyes glittered. "I'll raise the blasted roof if I must to get decent service."

Hesitating, the landlord glanced again at Molly, and she felt her appearance being weighed against how she must have sounded, for she had forgotten to use what she was now thinking of as her vulgar Sallie-voice.

Wiping his hands on his apron, the innkeep asked, "Wife is it?"

"Bride to be, actually. I'm taking her home to meet my family," Theo said. He lifted his chin and stared at the man, and Molly hoped she never earned such a cold gaze. Though it wasn't directed at her, she still shivered. "You may wish us happy, and then you may get us food and rooms. And a maid to take care of my lady-wife."

The innkeep rubbed his jaw, but still he did not give in, and Molly began to resign herself to a night in some hayfield.

Theo seemed to have other ideas. Pulling a silver card case from his waistcoat, he took out a thick, printed card and held it out, his expression now one of bored contempt. She caught sight of the elegant black script— *Theodore Basil Kendall Winslow, Winslow Park, Somerset.* Seven brief words, as if they were all needed for him to claim his place in the world. And they probably were.

Stepping forward, the innkeep took the card with a grimy, work-hardened hand and he held it between two fingers. He looked impressed, and as if he did not want to be, and he now eyed her, Molly noticed, as if he no longer knew what to think of her.

"Well, do you keep all your guests waiting in the hall?" Theo demanded.

Whether it was the card—a costly bit of extravagance well beyond the means of most folks, who put their money toward sensible food and clothing—or Theo's arrogance, the innkeep at last offered a curt bow. With one more suspicious glance at Molly, he offered to show them to their rooms himself and then he took up a candle from a side table and started up the stairs.

As soon as the innkeep turned his back, Theo shot Molly a grin and a wink.

"I wish we could stop elsewhere," she whispered to him, as they started up the shallow wooden stairs.

"Not a bit of it. Besides, if he insults you again I shall just pull out my pistols."

The innkeep shot them a startled glance, and when he turned away, Molly whispered to Theo, "You don't travel with pistols."

"Don't I just," he said, his eyes glittering wicked in the flickering light.

She shook her head, but then the innkeep was bowing them into two rooms at the top of the stairs with a cautious respect. "It's the best I've got left. Two pound eleven a night for both, paid in advance, and that'll include your dinner and breakfast tomorrow," he said, almost as if he begrudged every word.

Theo pulled out a coin, let the gold glitter in his fingers a moment and then he pressed it into the innkeeper's hand. "That's five guineas, so you may see to my horses and groom as well. And send up some warm water for the lady."

Bowing deeper now, the innkeep gave over the candle to Theo and hurried down the stairs.

"Money shouldn't make such a difference in

manners," Molly said, frowning as she watched their host hurry away.

Theo glanced at her. "Doesn't it make a difference in everything?"

She turned to him, ready to deny that it did, and then she realized how absurd it would be for her to argue such a thing when it was fifty pounds that had enticed her to go with him. And yet, it still did not feel as if money ought to make a difference in all matters.

However, he had a knowing look in his eyes, a gleam of awareness that he had backed her into a corner. He leaned closer. "Now, what is your preference?"

Her pulse skittered and she almost stepped back. "Preference?"

He grinned. "In rooms? So you might tidy up before we dine."

She glanced up at him, which set the feather on her bonnet to bobbing. Then she took the candle from him, careful not to touch her hand to his, and went into the nearest room.

Small but tidy, she thought. The bed smelled of rosewater and fresh air, no trace of mold. And soon enough a maid knocked on her door with a china pitcher of warm water and a matching basin, patterned with pink cabbage roses, and a cloth over her arm. A moment later another knock came, this one bringing one of the stable lads and Molly's trunk, which he placed on the floor near the narrow cot.

When he left, Molly took off her bonnet, undid her jacket, and pulled loose the lacing at the back of her gown and slipped it from her shoulders.

The evening was warm enough that the air felt cool on her skin as she stood about in nothing more than the linen of her chemise. She lay the dress upon a straight-backed wooden chair, splashed water on her face, and as she dried her skin she looked with longing at the bed.

She ought to comb the tangles from her curls. She ought to change into another dress for dinner. She ought not keep Theo waiting.

Instead she sat down on the bed—ah, it felt so good. Leaning over, she unlaced her half-boots and when her stocking-clad feet were free she wiggled her toes.

Would it hurt to just take five minutes for a lie down?

After all, would she not be far better company after a rest? And was it not part of tidying herself to do the inside as well as the outside?

With a guilty glance at the door, she stretched out on the narrow cot. Lumpy though the aged feather mattress was, she had never felt anything so heavenly.

She let go a sigh. And her eyes closed themselves.

Theo waited downstairs, but after two mugs of ale—a decent dark porter with a sharp tang to it—he decided to see what was keeping his sweet Molly Sweet. Lord, how that woman liked to keep a fellow waiting!

He took the stairs two at a time, and then stopped before her door, uncertain. Did he just open the door and enter? Or knock and wait for permission? Or should he even go into her room? He had bought her time, but he had also presented her to the innkeep as a respectable lady, and he was loath to do anything that might get them both tossed from the inn. He didn't fancy a night without a soft mattress under him.

Of course, if he could have something else soft underneath him, it might be worth it.

The image of Molly's lush figure pulled a smile from him and gave him encouragement enough. For the last five miles in the carriage, she had been brushing up against him—a touch of her shoulder against his, a rub of her cheek before she jerked upright, and even one sweet stroke of her breast against his arm. And he'd been unable to do anything since he had his hands full with four reins and two horses.

Not what a fellow really wanted to hold, blast it.

So why not see if he could now satisfy that ache she had stirred.

He knocked softly, then twisted the doorknob and found it yielding, so he stepped inside. He had not brought a candle with him, but one sputtered low in its holder on the dresser in Molly's room, giving a warm, yellow light to one corner of the room.

For an instant he almost thought she was not there, but then the candle flickered and he saw the white shape on the bed.

She lay curled on her side, one hand tucked under her chin, her chest rising and falling with the deep even breaths of sleep. Her curls tumbled loose and free, a glorious spill of red that cascaded over bare, white shoulders. She wore nothing but thin white linen, cut low and nearly transparent, riding high enough to show her legs up to the swell of her thigh.

Entranced, he stood in the doorway, blood heating and fast in his veins, tempted to shut the door behind them so he might join her in bed.

Then her mouth curved up. And, as he watched, she made a small happy sound and shifted ever so slightly, turning onto her back. His mouth dried as he took in the sight of those lovely breasts pushing against the thin fabric.

With a groan, he turned from the room and closed the door. Then he leaned there, eyes shut, still seeing her and aching to turn around and go back.

But—blast—she was supposed to be respectable here. And she looked so damnably comfortable. He had not the heart to wake her. Not for her dinner. And not for the hunger now stirring inside him.

Then the humor of it struck him and he opened his

eyes and grinned at himself. Blazes, he'd bought a woman he couldn't have! He damned well hoped Terrance would appreciate all he was going through.

Pushing away from her room—and the too sweet temptation inside—he started downstairs to at least claim his dinner. Another pint or two wouldn't diminish that delectable image of Molly Sweet in nothing more than her undergarments, but it would bloody well make it more bearable that he couldn't act on them tonight.

He would content himself with the thought of there always being another night to follow this one. And that a fellow ought to enjoy the chase of the hunt as much as he did the moment of glory that came at the end.

Crowing—raucous and far too energetic for the hour—woke Molly. Pulling open her eyes, she noted the gray light that filtered into her room from the single, small window. With a yawn, she sat up, pushed back her hair and peered about the room, wondering why it looked so odd.

Then she remembered.

She was not in her room at Sallie's house. She was not even in London. And she had slept through dinner, her empty, grumbling stomach reminded her. She covered her mouth for a moment, utterly mortified. Oh, she did so hope that Theo had not waited his own meal until it was too cold to eat. Well, nothing she could do about that.

And then she giggled. Here she had been worried about his taking advantage of her, and it seemed more apt to say that she had been doing nothing but taking advantage of his good nature.

Then she thought of his treatment of the innkeep.

No, he did not have quite that good a nature. She would have to remember that.

With a yawn, she stretched. Rising, she went to the

window to unlatch it and push open the hinged panes. She drew in a deep breath. Her childhood memories of morning were of spice-scented streets, of heat and moisture, and the wafting stench that came from the city of Madras when the wind changed. London, too, had its own unique scent—one of pungent coal fires, of horses in the streets, and of the Thames when the tide was low. But here, ah, here, the air smelled fresh with promise. Aromas of bread baking set her stomach rumbling— warm smells of yeast and milk and egg and flour.

Gracious, but she could eat a cow!

With a skip and a smile, she set to taking care of her body's needs. She washed with cold water, her skin tingling at its touch. Why had Theo not sent someone to wake her? Would he be angry with her for sleeping and not keeping him company? Or had he perhaps not even noticed her absence?

Still, he had paid for her to come with him to Somerset—not to entertain him, really. Just to be low.

With that in mind she glanced at the green and yellow striped dress she had worn yesterday. Shameful as it was, she still thought it most attractive. The bright colors reminded her of a bird's exotic plumage. And that was just what she was supposed to be—an exotic bird. A captive one, at that.

Then she remembered the lady.

How wonderful it would be to be so . . . so elegant.

Ah, well. Might as well wish for wings, there, too.

With that, she turned her attention away from useless feelings and into the tasks at hand. She had learned to do that years ago, when that had been the only way to survive a world turned terrifying.

Starting to hum, she dressed in the green and yellow again.

She struggled with the ties at the back, but finally got them done up. She left off the jacket, but a shawl from her trunk covered the loose lacing at the back anyway. And then she went downstairs to find herself the first guest to rise.

Her presence earned her suspicious stares from the innkeep and the plump, black-haired woman who looked to be his wife. But the woman brought her tea, and Molly asked about what might be for breakfast and if she had smelled cinnamon, and that got them started on food.

By the time Theo came downstairs to the main parlor, he found Molly seated with a stout, dark-haired woman, both of them drinking tea, the remains of breakfast on the polished pine table before them. Molly seemed to be writing something in a small book as the stout woman spoke, her Berkshire accent strong.

"Mind, now, use a good strong beer. Some hold as it's molasses you want, but I say treacle. Aye, and black pepper and allspice—fine ground, mind—for a stronger taste."

"And it's bay salt you use?"

"Aye. After the saltpetre finely beaten, mind."

"Saltpetre? What in blazes is that for?" Theo said, striding into the room.

Five

Both women rose, but Theo kept his eyes on his sweet Sweet. Only a redhead with that transparent skin, no matter how freckled, could redden with such a strong rush of color. It surprised him again that she could blush like a maiden. And left him uneasy. Was she new at her line of work, and still able to feel a sense of shame? That was not what he had wanted to hire.

She tried to tuck the small notebook behind her skirts, but he took her hand, asking, "What's this?"

Tugging her hand from his grasp, she glanced at the other woman. "Mrs. Weld, would you bring coffee and ale, and some more of that ham? Would you like bread and a toasting fork as well?" she said then, turning back to him, a smile in place, but also moving away from him, that book of hers now behind her skirts.

"Blazes take the toast. Beef and ale will do for me."

Mrs. Weld bobbed a curtsy and hurried away to bring the food, and Molly used the chance, he noticed, to place herself on the opposite side of the table from him. Well, at least she seemed to be something of a natural actress, for she was taking this acting like a lady quite seriously. Perhaps the crimson on her cheeks had been from the pleasure of seeing him—a nice thought that.

He leaned his palms on the back of a straight-backed wooden chair. "Well, my lady-wife, or soon to be so at least for my father's notice, you had best seat yourself, unless it's your wish I eat standing."

She sat down then, and he did the same, eyeing the book that she had in her lap now. "And what in blazes were you writing?" He frowned as a thought struck. "You aren't one of those bookish types who go about taking down everything everyone says in some ghastly diary?"

Stiffening, she glared at him as if he had insulted her. "Bookish? Certainly not. And all I was taking down was Mrs. Weld's recipe for smoking ham. If you had some yourself, you'd see why I asked for it."

Eyes narrowed, he stared at her. *Ham?* Why in blazes would a strumpet care about ham? Or was she making some sort of ribald play on words? If she was, it certainly hadn't come with any suggestive looks. So that led him back to wondering why a bird of paradise, such as her, would care about ham?

Her nose wrinkled, and then she said, her tone clipped, "Do you think a woman of easy virtue to be a woman of no virtue at all? I'll have you know that all Sallie's girls can set a tidy stitch, and they at least know how to boil water for tea. Do you think they—we all sit about thinking only of . . . of . . . of cavorting?"

He grinned. "Cavorting? Come now, why not use a nice old Anglo-Saxon word for it? Or don't you like to be blunt about your trade?"

She blushed fiercer than before. "Even a working girl has to consider domestic necessities."

"Such as recipes?"

"I like food," she said, her chin lifting and her green eyes glittering hot.

His let his glance stray to her plump curves. "Well, you need not eat me. I've nothing to complain of in that. I like a girl with a healthy appetite." His grin widened, and he turned as the innkeeper's wife came back, a tray in hand with a platter of cold beef and a pewter mug of ale.

"Speaking of such—Mrs. Weld, you are an angel to be so prompt. And my Molly tells me I must try some of your ham."

Molly watched him charm her and flirt with inkeeper's wife until he had her blushing as well, and giving his hand a playful slap before she left to fetch for him. That smile of his, Molly decided, probably got him his way in most things. That and those dark, dramatic looks of his. But when he grinned, his expression did away with the soulful, romantic impression stirred by that handsome face, the one that made him look angelic.

Dangerously so.

It would be a mistake, she knew, to ever think this one an innocent lad.

Almost as if reading her thoughts, he winked at her over his tankard of ale. It was as if a hand clenched around her throat. She glanced away, face warm. This whole adventure might have been easier had he been as unappealing as the florid banker that Sallie had once introduced to her. Of course, it would not have been as much fun. Nor would she have taken it on.

Her lips curved up.

My Molly.

How nice that sounded. But she really must remember that she was his only because of the fifty pounds he had paid for her. No, not for her. For her time, she amended. Just as Sallie paid for her time and cooking. Even so, she squirmed in her chair. There seemed to be far too thin a line between selling her body to him for his pleasure, and selling herself to him as a pretend wife.

Still, that line existed. Or at least she hoped it did, for about all she had left to anchor herself in this world was her self-respect.

When he finished his ham and beef, and had praised both to Mrs. Weld, he suggested a stroll along Hungerford's streets, saying, "We've time before the horses are harnessed."

Molly agreed at once. Anything to delay another full day of that rocking carriage. Going upstairs, she put on her bonnet, Spencer jacket and gloves, then came downstairs to find him waiting, his tall beaver-skin at a jaunty angle.

The town was still waking, but Molly soon found herself uncomfortable with the stares she drew from those residents and shopkeepers who were abroad. She had forgotten her status again, as a less than respectable woman.

By the time Theo handed her into his brother's curricle, she found herself eager to leave. Gracious, but it would also be good when this finished and she could slip into in her own plain muslin gowns again—and she vowed never to think them so dowdy or wish for something a bit brighter.

The warm weather held, with a bright sky and not enough clouds to worry over rain. That left the roads dusty still, but Molly was too interested in the scenery to care. She spent her time asking Theo of the landmarks they passed, but he had no idea about their names or histories. Often enough, Burke leaned forward to give her an answer, his tone churlish enough that Theo would then rebuke him, and the two would set to arguing almost like boys over Burke's lack of respect.

The further they traveled, however, the more Theo's answers changed into curt replies, and the more he began to look like a gloomy poet. He even stopped replying to any barbs from his brother's groom, and his distracted frown began to wear on Molly, setting her to pulling at the tips of her gloves.

Across the downs near Cherril, Molly glimpsed a view of a giant white horse laid out in what seemed to be chalk on the green hillside. But Theo only stared at the road ahead, black eyebrows lowered into a flat line, his mouth tight and a hard look in his eyes, so she did not ask about it.

Finally, Molly ran out of patience and bluntly asked, "Are you going to brood the rest of the way there?"

Burke offered a snort of what might have been amusement, but Theo only glanced at her, then focused on his horses and the road again, keeping the pair to a steady trot. "I'm not brooding—I'm thinking."

"Worrying more like. And it's starting me to worry. Are you having second thoughts on this?"

"I should think so," Burke muttered.

Theo's jaw tightened so that she saw the pulse beating fast near his ear. "What you think wasn't asked for." He threw a glance over his shoulder to Burke, and then looked at Molly. "And I am not changing my mind about anything. I'm going to put a stop to this nonsense once and for all."

She slanted a look at him. He had not sounded as if his temper was meant for her, and she almost asked what nonsense he meant, only that look in his eyes—like thick ice—had her remembering the overbearing stare he had given the innkeep. So she asked instead, "Perhaps you ought to give me a better idea of what to expect? Preparation is half any job."

Glancing at her, his mouth quirked in a crooked half-smile, but the expression did not quite warm his eyes. "Now you sound like an actress."

She thought of the orchestrated meals she had had to arrange for the visit of two royal dukes to Sallie's house, and the other special affairs that had been held for the more select company that had visited. "We all perform in our own ways, don't we, ducks? Like me just now."

"She's got a point there," Burke said, leaning forward.

Theo threw a sharp stare at him. "You may be Terrance's groom, but don't think I won't set you down so that you can walk the rest of the way."

Muttering, Burke sat back, arms crossed. Theo turned to Molly. "And you . . . you know all you need to know. Just act smitten and. . . ."

"And vulgar. Yes, so you've said already. But I'm not the one who needs to act smitten, now am I? Seems to me that would do better as your role."

The act of overtaking a wagon piled high with hay took his concentration. When they were past, he steadied the pair and demanded, "Just how do you figure that?"

Molly warmed to her idea, and slipped more into Sallie's accent. "Well, think on it, ducks. You're the one bringin' me home. Why else would you unless you can't stand to have me out of your sight? So, seems as if that ought to be due to your being smitten blind. Ready to do whatever I ask, in fact."

"And you'd enjoy that, would you?" he asked, voice dry.

She wrinkled her nose. "I doubt we're talking much pleasure for me in this. You've been brooding enough. . . ."

"I don't brood!"

". . . brooding enough," she said firmly, "that I can only think the welcome we'll get from your father will be colder than an East wind off the Thames in a wet January."

Theo's mouth twisted.

But it was Burke who answered, his tone insolent as ever. "Not cold, miss. It's a hot temper all the Winslows have. The squire'll most likely strip the walls with his cursing."

"Well, that does sound a right treat for me, now doesn't it. And just what else might he do?" She rounded on Theo. "Here now—he's not the type to do more than shout, is he?"

Theo glanced at her, blue eyes blazing. "As in what? Box your ears or mine? Take a whip to us? He may have the Winslow temper, but he's not a savage! And Burke, if you say one thing more without being asked, you will be walking! Blazes—as if I'd pull any female into a dicey situation!"

She bit her lower lip to stop the apology from slipping out, then muttered, "Well, it's not as if I know much of anything about you, now do I?"

His mouth tightened. "You know enough."

She stared at his hard-set jaw for a moment—a stubborn profile, she decided, what with those dark brows flat over his eyes and a deep furrow between them. Now she knew how he got those lines in his forehead.

For once, Burke also kept his tongue between his teeth. He, too, must have heard that implacable tone in Theo's voice.

Turning to face the road again, she let out a sigh. "I suppose I do."

For a moment only the beat of hooves on the road carried to them, and the breeze from the brisk moving carriage whispered across her ears. Then Theo said, his voice almost accusing, "Now *you're* going to brood."

She lifted one shoulder. "Over what? I know well enough what to do, so it seems we have little else to say."

At the sound of galloping hooves on the hard road behind him, Theo eased the curricle to one side. The mail coach—for Bath he guessed—galloped past in dust and shouts from the driver, the passengers on the roof clinging to the railing that surrounded the seats on the top of the coach and to their hats.

He glanced down at his own passenger. He could barely see the tip of her pert nose just now—that damn bonnet of hers. He waited for some other comment from her, some new question. He hadn't bargained for such an inquisitive woman, but that's what came of looking for a brazen hussy, he supposed. He had wanted a woman with no sensibilities—no delicate feelings that could be easily bruised.

Well, perhaps he could satisfy a little of her infernal curiosity.

"It's simple, you know. All you need to do is be brass,

solid through. My father will tear into me—not you. Least that's what I'm expecting—what I want, in fact. It's past time he learned I'm done dancing to his tunes. So when he starts to yell, just clutch at me and let me do all the talking. He's a crusty old devil, but he's been that way since my mother died, though I seem to recall he shouted even before then. Only this time, I'm going to make damn certain he has something to honestly shout about."

They drove straight through Bath, quite the most elegant city, Molly decided. With its buildings of white stone, it fairly gleamed, nestled against the rolling, green hills. She wished they might stop for tea and a rest. The shops, with their lovely bow windows to display fabrics and Bath buns, and teas and books, stirred a longing in her to browse along the streets. But Theo kept the horses to a brisk trot, navigating the traffic of other carriages and strolling elegant ladies and gentlemen with ease.

He allowed a short stop in Dunkerton at The Swan for a meal and a change of horses, and at that point Molly thought she would have eaten anything put before her— even the ghastly meat pie she had left behind the day before. However, The Swan provided a lovely summer Pease soup, mutton, macaroni, and a vegetable pie, followed by the thickest strawberry jam, the lightest scones, and the smoothest Devon cream that Molly had ever tasted. She wanted to ask for the recipes for all, but Theo hurried her out so fast she barely had time to pop the last luscious bite of scone into her mouth.

Not long after, the countryside opened into flat land, with only one towering hill to be noted.

"That's the Tor—Glastonbury Tor," Burke answered to her question about it.

Theo merely kept driving.

After yet another village, Molly began to be just a little

bored by the trees and fields, cows and sheep. The road had narrowed to more of a lane—they must have turned from the main road—and tension had tightened lines around Theo's mouth.

"Will we be there soon?" she asked, hungry again despite having eaten her fill earlier. The sun lay low on the horizon, but there would be another few hours of light. A full moon also showed a pale face in the eastern sky.

"Soon enough," he said.

Molly gave an inward sigh. It might be awful to face his father, but at this stage she would rather face any number of irate gentlemen—just so long as she could step out of this rocking carriage.

They skimmed through a lovely, tidy village, but it was growing too dark for Molly to see much of it, other than thatched roofs on some of the cottages and lighted windows. She glanced longingly at the sign for The Four Feathers with the warm glow of light in the inn's mullioned windows, but Theo did not check his pace.

Not long after, he slowed the carriage and turned at a gated drive.

Molly sat up, fatigue almost forgotten.

She glanced at Theo. The gathering dusk made it more difficult to see his face—and they were in a shaded drive just now—but she thought she saw that same stubborn jut to his chin.

And then the drive curved, and the lights from the house ahead of them caught her attention.

House? Manor, more like. A lovely one at that.

Perched as it was on a small rise, the house caught the last of the light, some of the second story windows winking silver, and the last of the sunset gave a mellow warmth to the stone walls. A gabled roof stretched up in tidy peaks over stone walls that looked as if they had been there forever.

Pleasure warmed her at the thought of how wonderful it must be to know that such a house always waited your return.

She shot a worried glance at Theo. How could he bear to court banishment from this place? But perhaps it meant nothing to him. Or perhaps he had somewhere else better to go.

And then her mind turned to practical questions. "Theo, if your father throws us out tonight, where are we to sleep?"

He glanced at her, then answered, sounding a little put out, and very much as if he had not thought of this before, "We'll stay in Halsage—there's usually rooms for let."

She hoped that would prove true. She did not fancy more miles of traveling, particularly by night, no matter how bright the moon.

Gravel crunched under the horses' hooves, and then the carriage wheels swept across the drive before Theo pulled the pair of grays harnessed to the curricle to a halt.

Jumping down, Burke hurried to hold the horses' heads, but Theo sat for a moment, staring up at the house.

It's not too late. Molly willed the thoughts from her head to his, hoping he might indeed turn away. To throw away this as his inheritance—oh, he must indeed be a little unbalanced to do such a thing.

Or perhaps he just had his reasons. Perhaps she had been blessed in never having had close kin.

Turning in his seat, the curricle rocked as he shifted his weight, then he asked, his tone a touch uncertain now, "You ready?"

She nodded, then realized he might not see such a gesture. So she put up her chin. "Ready as I'll ever be, ducks. Besides, anything that gets me to a hot cup of tea within the hour is good enough by me."

His grin flashed in the gathering twilight. "You were a good choice," he said. His finger flicked under her chin, then he jumped down and held up his arms to help her.

With her feet on the ground again, Molly could swear she still felt the sway of the carriage. Her heart also picked up a sickening pace as she glanced at the house.

Theo's voice, now strong and set, gave her courage. "Walk 'em Burke. We won't be long."

"I hope not," Molly muttered. The shorter the better.

"This is where you earn your money," he said, then he offered his arm. "Shall we beard the lion in his den?"

She put her hand on his arm. "The only lions I've ever seen are at the Tower, and they're toothless, old mangy things."

He grinned again. "This one isn't toothless or mangy, but let's hope he gets his roaring done fast."

Leading the way, he ran up the steps and Molly kept pace with him. He didn't bother to knock, but reached to open the door only to have it swing open before him.

"Hallo, Simpson," he said, his tone brazen now.

The older servant fell back a step. "Master Theo? We hadn't expected you!" His stare traveled to Molly. He held a lamp in one hand and had opened the door with the other. The light cascaded across Molly, and Theo glanced at her.

The ostrich feathers on her bonnet might be wilting, but she had pasted a smile in place and those green eyes of hers sparkled with a militant challenge. Admiration for her rose in him. By all, he had seen some real luck in finding her.

As Simpson—his father's butler—stepped back, startled enough that he had allowed the shock to register with a slack jaw and glassy eyes, Molly swept into the house.

She paused in the hallway and started looking about her as if pricing every item, from the tapestries on the walls, to the tables, to the chairs that had been around since the Crusades.

Theo fought down a grin at that, and then turned to Simpson. "This is Molly Sweet. She's to have the Queen's Bedchamber."

At that Molly swung around, her eyes wide. But she seemed to recover for she offered up a smile, then said, "Lordy, ducks. You said you'd treat me right proper like a queen."

London Cockney now dripped from her voice, and Theo had to resist another smile. Blazes, but she would give his father an apoplexy! Grim satisfaction settled into him. About time his father learned that he had two grown sons—and not puppets he could make dance to any whim!

Simpson had recovered his customary wooden face. The man never aged, Theo thought. He had been in the squire's service for as long as Theo could recall and had always had that lantern jaw, silver-streaked thinning black hair, and narrow shoulders that were stooped with age. Nothing got under Simpson's skin—not years, and not even a strumpet in a green and yellow striped dress who was expected to sleep in the same bedchamber that had once housed Queen Elizabeth.

Well, he'd soon see about that. He glanced around him. "And you can tell my father, Simpson, that we have a guest."

"Beg pardon, but I cannot, sir."

Theo stared at the man. "Cannot? Why in blazes not?"

Simpson blinked, then said, his tone perfectly bland, "The squire is not at home."

Six

Eyes narrowed, Theo stared at Simpson, trying to see behind the polite phrase. The words were used often enough as an excuse to avoid unwelcome visitors. The squire, however, scorned such diplomatic evasions—if he did not want to see someone he told them so, blunt as a hammer wrapped in plain cloth.

"Where in blazes is he if not here?" Theo asked, biting off the words as he tried to curb his annoyance.

Simpson closed the front door. "I cannot say, sir. He left the day before yesterday. Something about a horse, I believe."

"It would be," Theo muttered. The squire had always paid more heed to his hunters and race horses than he had to anything else in his life. Typical of the man not to be here now he was wanted. "Well, how am I to—?"

He checked his own words for he had been about to say more than was wise—Simpson was his father's servant after all. Instead, he decided he might as well start the game, so he added, "How am I to present my bride to him?"

Shock glittered in Simpson's light brown eyes and slackened his jaw. His glance slipped to Molly, and then he dragged his stare from her, stiffening again into starched propriety.

Least I got a reaction from him about something, Theo thought, though he found less satisfaction in achieving that long-sought goal than he had ever expected. It had only taken his entire twenty-five years to get past the man's inhuman restraint. But it would have been more fun to do so when it wasn't his future and Terrance's that were being staked on the outcome of how this particular hand was played.

Theo glanced at Molly, who gazed back at him, an expectant look in her green eyes as if to ask, *"Now what?"* Good question, that. Lord, the situation would be laughable if it was not so damn irritating.

Glancing at Simpson again, he asked, "When do you expect his return?"

Uncertainty came into Simpson's eyes and he started to offer more vague politeness. Theo cut him off with a wave. "You don't know that either, do you? Of course not. Why would he tell anyone anything about his affairs! Well, at least you know the way to the Queen's room—and I hope you know enough to arrange dinner for us."

Hesitating, Simpson shot another glance at Molly, and then seemed to resign himself to the situation for he offered a bow and then started up the stairs, saying to Molly, his tone frigid, "This way, Miss Sweet."

Molly sent Theo a questioning stare, as if she was not the least comfortable about any of this, but at his nod of encouragement, she gave a small shrug, then turned and started up the stairs after Simpson. Frowning, Theo watched her.

Blazes, but this put a branch in the spokes of everything. How did he now convince Molly to stay until his father should return? And what in blazes would he do if the squire stayed away for more than a fortnight?

Resisting the urge to ask questions about the house— which seemed heavy with history and stories—Molly followed the butler up the thickly carpeted stairs that creaked with age under her steps. The house seemed to be all stairs and hallway, wood wainscoting, and plastered walls painted in dark greens and reds and hung with portraits of horses or dogs or people in lace or satin or both.

It was enough to intimidate anyone. Or at least anyone who hadn't also seen the white marble palaces of India's powerful rajahs, with peacocks strutting the halls, and gold-clad slaves, and enough opulence to truly awe.

So she merely looked about herself.

Silent disapproval emanated from the butler's stiff form as he opened a heavy oak door into a bedroom and then went about the act of using a spill of wood, lit by his lamp, to light the candles.

Molly glanced around the room as it moved from shadow to light, and she found herself a touch disappointed.

Paneled in dark wood, the chamber did not quite fit her idea of housing for a queen. In India, a queen would have had a cavern of a room—or at least that's how her childhood memories painted the image of the great palace she had once visited in Madras.

In this room, heavy red drapery hung from two sets of windows. Three dark paintings of indistinct hunting scenes and horses hung on the wall, and the furnishings—a maple wardrobe and dressing table, and two high-backed wooden chairs—looked as rigid as the butler and just as uncomfortable. The only lightness came from an intricately plastered white ceiling; the enormous bed, with its red brocade tester and hangings, was the only thing that resembled luxury.

"You don't mean to say a queen slept in this tiny hole of a room, do you?" she asked, remembering to keep her Sallie voice in place and simply allowing the thoughts in her head to tumble out uncensored.

Simpson stared at her, his face puckering as if he had bitten into an unripe gooseberry. "This is the Tudor wing of the house. Rooms were built small and paneled for warmth."

"Didn't they think a nice cheerful fire could do just as well? But I s'pose the bed's a bit of all right."

The corner of his mouth twitched and not with a smile. "I shall see your things are brought up and that a maid is sent to attend you."

With another curt bow, one that managed to convey ironic disdain, he left. When the door shut, Molly let out a breath. "Coo, but he's got to be worse than the squire," she muttered. And then she giggled. She had sounded more like Sallie than even Sallie ever did.

Gracious, but would she have a story to tell when she returned. That set her frowning. Just when she would return now seemed to be in question. And while a few weeks of holiday might be fun in other circumstances, she wondered if so much time away might put it into Sallie's head to hire another cook. Sallie's good nature only stretched so far, after all.

Well, at dinner she would make clear to Theo that she could allow him no more than a few days leeway. That seemed fair enough. In the meantime, she knew how to take a blessing as it came. And she was happy enough not to have to meet the squire tonight—travel weary, hungry, and rumpled.

Taking off her jacket and her shoes, she let her thoughts wander ahead to the pleasure of washing the dust from her face, of slipping into a fresh gown and sitting down to a hot meal. That seemed close enough to paradise just now.

Thankfully, her trunk came up on the back of a footman soon enough. He seemed inclined to linger, a rather cheeky grin in place, so she sent him away. Then a maid brought her hot water—and stayed to gawk. No sooner had that one been dismissed than another knocked on the door to ask Molly if she needed anything. One more then arrived after that—gracious, but they had servants to spare—to lead her to the drawing room, saying that Mr. Winslow waited on her company for dinner.

And now I know exactly how those poor old lions in the Tower menagerie feel, Molly thought, walking down the hall behind the maid, who kept sliding curious glances back at her. *They all want to see what Theo's brought home for a bride—and I had best give them a show for that's what I'm here for.*

So she put on a broad smile and asked if the paintings were of any real value, and wondered how much had been paid for the vases, chairs, and side tables they passed, and speculated on how much each might fetch at auction. That earned her appalled, wide-eyed stares from the maid, and Molly almost wanted to reassure the girl that she actually really did not mean any of it.

Only she had a role to play. And, in truth, she found a giddy, secret delight in saying anything that came into her head. Perhaps Theo had been right and there was a bit of actress in her. Or perhaps it was just the sense of freedom it brought.

Since she had been left alone on the London docks at twelve, survival had meant learning how best to please others. She had become quite good at that, and had found a measure of satisfaction in such a skill. However, with it came the pressure that failure meant beatings and starving and cold rooms without a light or a blanket. She had learned that well at the workhouse. That had changed with Sallie, but the training had stuck. Now, she was turned loose. She was supposed not to please—so she could say what she wanted, and, oh, gracious, was that not a treat.

Of course, it also helped to know she would be there only a day or two, and so need not deal with the consequences of stirring up everyone's animosity. Which was another good reason to make certain her stay would be a short one.

In the drawing room, she found Theo still in his traveling clothes—buff breeches, black boots, white shirt with a spotted handkerchief knotted about his throat instead of a proper cravat, and a buff waistcoat. He had at least changed his coat—a blue one for a brown one.

He gave her an approving stare. She had dressed in a vivid red silk evening gown taken from Jane's wardrobe. The hem had had to be pinned up, which one of the maids had done without a question as to why Molly should own a dress that did not fit her. Cut low, the dress showed the swell of her breasts, pushing them up in a rather shocking fashion, and the color rather clashed with her hair and her freckles. But she rather thought she looked just as she ought: like one of Sallie's girls.

However, she was not about to be alone in this Maygame of his, so she raked a critical stare over Theo as soon as they were alone. "I rate a new coat, but not more? That's not what I call gentlemanly, nor very like to seem as if you wish to impress me."

He frowned at her as if she had just kicked him. "You never complained before."

"That was on the road. And we may not have your father here to watch, but we have every other pair of eyes in this house." She smiled at him. "Or don't you want them thinking you're really courting me?"

"Oh, for. . . ." He lifted one hand with exasperation. "That means putting dinner back, you know."

She sat down on a silk-covered chair. "As if I could eat much with a black-spotted, mustard yellow kerchief opposite me."

He glowered at her, and she answered with lifted brows and a calm face. Turning, he stalked from the room.

A quarter hour later he returned, now in a black coat and knee breeches, white stockings and black patent shoes, a white cravat neatly tied, and a cream satin waist-coat embroidered with vivid peacock colors. He looked devastatingly handsome, and she could almost wish she had not asked him to change. Her mouth dried and her pulse lifted as he came to her, blue eyes sparkling as if he planned to extract a suitable revenge for being made to dress.

Gracious, but he'd turn any girl's head, looking as he did.

Rising, she pulled her own white wool shawl up from where it had dropped to her elbows and took up the attack before he could. "Don't you ever brush your hair?"

He glanced up as if to see the spill of black hair over his eyes, then he brushed at it, disordered the careless locks even more. "There—that do for you?"

With a shake of her head, she came closer. "You must have driven your mother mad." Standing on tiptoe, she ran her fingers though the dark locks.

Soft as corn silk, it wound around her fingers. She had not worn gloves—she owned not a single pair suitable for evening, and there had been none in Jane's left-behind clothing. Now she could only be glad of such a thing. How could a man's hair wrap around a girl's fingers almost as if to tangle her touch so she'd never be able to pull away?

He stared down at her, the blue deepening so that it looked like twilight in his eyes. Voice rough and low, he asked, "Do you do this for all your gentlemen?"

Jerking her hand away, Molly moved toward the door, fussing with her shawl.

Theo mentally kicked himself for blundering. Why had he said anything? Why had he not just kissed her as he had wanted? All he would have had to do is reach out a hand and snag her closer. Instead, he had opened his mouth and reminded her of her hired status.

Cheeks now a warm pink, she gave him a bright, careless smile over one white shoulder. "Can we eat now? I'm famished."

Well, no kisses for him tonight. She had gone and put distance between them again, and she looked as if she had every intent to keep him to that blasted agreement they had made.

Blazes, why had he ever said he would act the gentleman with her? She looked an utter treat in that gown.

Offering his arm, he led her to the dining room.

Simpson would have stayed to supervise the meal, with two footmen to help, if Theo had allowed it. The butler would also have seated them at opposite sides of the table, but Theo put a stop to that as well, insisting the place settings be moved to a corner of the table in close proximity. Then he asked that the dishes be set out now.

"I'll ring for you to clear the course," he said. And let them all think the worst—it would both reinforce the idea that Molly was leading him astray to dine in such an informal fashion, and it would give him a chance to regain some ground with her. And perhaps get that kiss he wanted.

Simpson's face had acquired a pinched look, as if his drawers had suddenly shrunk to half their size, but he bowed and moved at once to obey Theo's orders.

As soon as he left, Molly leaned closer. "Thank you— I was wondering how I could eat anything with them staring at me."

He turned to her, a little surprised she should be so sensitive. "Why shouldn't they stare—you're a beautiful woman."

Pleasure rushed into her face, lighting her eyes and her smile. He decided then and there to dedicate the rest of the meal to earning more smiles from her.

He entertained her with stories about Simpson, and the exploits he and Terrance had undertaken to rattle the maddeningly placid butler. "He never did more than say, 'Very good, sir.' Or, 'Will that be all, sir?' Never so much as hinted at a rebuke to us—not even the time we set a bucket of eels loose in his bed."

Molly shuddered. "Eels! And your father never said anything?"

"Actually, he laughed at most of it. Except for the eels. He said it was a sin to waste God's creatures on a prank and gave us a suitable punishment."

She pulled back. "Did he cane you?"

"Oh, no. Far worse. He made us eat every last one of those eels. All at the same meal. We had fried eels, boiled eels, and eel soup for starters. Collared eels, stewed eels, eels and mushrooms, and eel pie. I can't even smell the things cooking now without wanting to turn tail and run."

She laughed, then said, "Well, now I know what never to cook for you."

"Ah, so that is why you collect recipes—you cook. Why in blazes do you do that? Doesn't Sallie at least employ servants for you?"

Taking up her wine, Molly took a large sip of the woody burgundy and regarded him over the brim. He already thought her low, and she could well imagine that if she admitted to being a cook in a brothel he would be horrified to find she was but a mere servant to the lowest of the low. A cook in a bawdy house. Gracious, he also might send her packing without her fifty pounds.

So she only smiled. "That's my secret, ducks. A woman, after all, must have some mystery."

She had often heard Sallie say such a thing, and she still had no idea what it meant really. But just now it suited her needs perfectly. Then she asked, keeping her tone pert, "Do you take your port alone, or will you give me a game of backgammon?" She had noticed the board in the drawing room—a lovely set with smooth ivory pieces and half the markers stained black.

"You play?" he asked, rising and then moving to pull back her chair.

She straightened and said, her tone proud, "I was taught by none other than the Rajah of Tanjore."

He laughed. "Were you now? Well, that sounds a challenge to me."

In the drawing room, they moved the board nearer to the window, for the evening was fine, and Theo soon found that she played like a fiend. He didn't know about that story of a rajah teaching her—that sounded suspiciously like some invented tale. But when he found himself being trounced, he started to play as he would against Terrance or his father rather than as he would against any lady of his acquaintance.

She beat him soundly.

As she swept her last piece off the board, he frowned and said at once, "Best of three."

She smiled. "Very well. But I warn you, the rajah taught me never to give any quarter in backgammon."

He glanced at her, eyes narrowed. A nonsense story, of course. Or perhaps there was something to these tales of a childhood in India—in fact, perhaps she had started her profession there. Could this rajah have taught her other things?

He found himself frowning at such an idea, even though it set his imagination wandering to what she might have learned of other Eastern arts. And that pulled his mind utterly away from this game.

She beat him again, but far less handily.

"Three out of five," he said, now scowling at the board.

Laughing, she threw up her hands. "Ah, no. The rajah also taught me to quit while I was ahead."

"But you must give me a rematch. Tomorrow evening, then."

The laugher died in her eyes. "What if your father returns before then?"

The light mood died in an instant. And Theo had only himself to blame for his unthinking comment on the uncertain future before them both. Rising, he began to set the backgammon pieces into the starting order for a game. "I spoke to Burke before dinner and the gossip he had from the stables is that it's likely the squire will be away at least a week."

"A week!" Molly stood now, her expression distressed. "But I can't stay that long. I have—well, I have work."

He glared at her. "And this isn't? You're being handsomely paid, and for precious little, I may say. And the agreement was that I've got to be disowned for you to earn your full fee." His frown changed suddenly to a beguiling smile. "Come now, you can't want to go back to London with me left unsatisfied. And you might actually find time to enjoy yourself here."

She folded her arms. "How am I to do that with every servant in this household watching as if I were some wild animal you brought home which they dare not trust?"

"Do they really? Well, if that's the case, take long walks. Or, better still, ride with me."

"On a horse?" she asked, anxiety suddenly squeaking in her voice.

He grinned. "That's the usual way, though I suppose I could find you a donkey. Or a nice round pony to fit your legs?"

She glared at him. "I'm not that small, thank you. And perhaps it is not that I am so short, it's just that you need trimming down to size!"

His grin widened as he thought of this pocket amazon taking him on. "Well, we could wrestle for it—I shouldn't mind. But I already told Sallie that this could take a while, and if you're all that worried about her kicking up a fuss, I'll send off some sort of note telling her to expect your return when she sees you."

She hesitated, and he leapt on the wavering indecision

he glimpsed in her eyes. As he did, he realized that there could be some lovely side benefits to having her stay an extra few days. Just one of them lay before him in the view offered by that low cut gown of hers.

Tone dropping low, he asked, "Have you ever seen Somerset? It's the best part of England, I swear. I'll show you about. Take you to the cathedral in Wells, if you fancy it. We could go on a picnic even, if we get a nice enough day for it."

"A picnic?"

He smiled at the wistful tone in her voice. "What? Haven't you ever been on a picnic?" She shook her head, her red curls swaying, glinting with gold threads in the candlelight. "Well, that must simply be remedied at once, Miss Sweet. It's obvious now that you must stay. And don't worry, the squire will be home soon enough."

She frowned at him. "I suppose I can't walk back to London. But, mind you, I can't stay here forever either!"

Grinning, he grasped her hand. "It's not forever, my sweet Sweet. But I swear it'll be a pleasant few days."

With a sigh, she shook her head. "You're a wicked man, I fear—you make me forget every good intention I have."

His grip tightened on her fingers. "Every one of them?"

She pulled her hand away. "That's not an intention I ever had with you."

"What isn't?" he asked, all innocence now.

But Molly only shook her head, refusing to answer him, and then she wished him a good night. And she fled before she started toying with the idea of how pleasant it would be to do more than she did intend with him.

True to his word, Theo started to show her about on the following day. He tried to convince her that such a perfect summer day, with the promise of heat in the air and a blue sky, called for ambling the neighborhood on horseback. However, she flatly refused his offer of the most placid mount.

"I haven't a riding habit, and don't you go offering to pay for one for me. If I ride and find I like it, then I'd miss it back in London. And if I don't like it, what's the point?"

He grinned at this logic, but gave in to her, settling instead for a walk under the lanes shaded by avenues of apple trees. This suited her quite well, and she found him surprisingly knowledgeable about the crops planted in the fields.

"Why do you not want to inherit this?" she asked, unable to understand and unable to keep the question inside.

He did not look down at her, but stopped in the lane and stared at the field next to them where tall, slender stalks of wheat swayed in the breeze.

"Because it's not mine. Terrance is the elder. It's his." He looked down at her and she was surprised to note how serious he seemed. How intent. "Blazes, if it were mine, I'd fight the devil himself to keep it. How could I rob my own brother of that?"

She had no answer for him. Only more questions.

Before she could ask about the tangle that seemed to be his family, the jingle of harness and the steady clop-clop beat of hooves on the hard dirt road told of a carriage approaching.

As an open landau came into view with what seemed to be a lady and a gentleman seated inside, Theo moved with her to the verge of the road to allow the carriage to pass. But as it drew near, the lady's voice rose, betraying both age and agitation, "Stop! Stop the coach, Fields. Amy! My dear, dearest sister!"

Startled, Molly looked up, and then she heard Theo swear under his breath. "Blast all! Lady Thorpe." He leaned closer. "Just smile and agree with whoever she takes you for or we shall be here all day arguing it."

"Whoever?" Molly asked, then she turned back to the coach, not understanding anything of what was going on.

As ordered, the coachman had halted the pair of dark brown horses that pulled the open landau and now Molly could see the passengers clearly.

The gentleman in the carriage seemed quite young— young enough to be the lady's son? Oddly, however, he dressed more like a servant, for his black coat and knee breeches and his white shirt, cravat, and waistcoat seemed more like plain livery than a gentleman's clothes. Molly turned her attention to the lady, who struggled with shaking hands to hold up a pair of eye-glasses from where they dangled on a golden chain around her neck.

She looks a tiny bird of a lady, Molly thought. Gray hair was swept up under an old fashioned straw bonnet that tied under the lady's chin with a pink ribbon. A pink sash decorated her white muslin gown and a ruffled white scarf lay around her neck, with the ends tucked into the pink sash at the high waist. Clothes really more suitable to a girl than a matron, but Molly found the picture charming.

Then clear gray eyes lifted and regarded her through the lorgnette glasses, its gold chain glittering as the sun drifted through the tree leaves.

Lady Thorpe's smile faded into sagging, parched skin. "Why, why, you're not Amy!"

The words came out almost accusingly.

Theo stepped forward and said firmly, as if speaking to a child, "Lady Thorpe, may I present Miss Molly Sweet."

She glanced at him and the smile lit her faded eyes again, brightening them, lifting her face again from the sagging wrinkles. "Ah, Lord Howe, how nice to see you."

Molly frowned. She shot a look at Theo. Was he really

a lord? Had he been less than honest about his identity? But his father's servants had not addressed him as if he were titled.

Lady Thorpe's voice drew her attention back, for the older woman suddenly announced, her tone commanding, "You're not Amy! Amy's dead. I remember now."

She glared at Molly for a moment as if somehow it was her fault that she was not Amy. But then her face lightened again. "Oh, but of course—you must be Amy's daughter! Yes. That's it! You must be my niece Mary all grown up!"

Seven

A shiver skittered through Molly, and aching desire spread after it. Could it be possible? Just perhaps? Her mother's name had been Amelia, not Amy. Still, that was close. And while she had never been called anything but Molly, was that not sometimes the pet name for Mary?

Gracious, it seemed impossible, yet Molly's mind spun with dazzling visions of having found relatives. Would that not be the most outlandish coincidence—or, perhaps, as the Hindu said, perhaps karma had led her here?

Only she knew that she wanted this too much—was too willing to believe. She wanted to be this woman's niece. To be anyone's niece. Or a sister, or cousin, or just related in some fashion. To no longer be alone in the world.

A lovely fantasy, but practical sense, earned with long years in a harsh world, told her to be sensible.

Still, that tantalizing hope persisted in her, beating wildly in her pulse.

"It's Molly, my lady. Molly Sweet," she said, stressing her name, more to herself than to anyone else.

Lady Thorpe beamed at her as if she had not even spoken. "Ah, Mary, you look so like your mother."

Molly's heart twisted and that flicker of hope spiraled into a warm blaze. Oh, but how she wanted this woman to be her aunt. Could it be possible?

She glanced at Theo, instinctively seeking reassurance from him that she was not fooling herself. Only what had he said? Something about agreeing to whoever Lady Thorpe took her to be?

Was this all some silly jest?

The hope twisted again inside her, this time into something desperate.

She had thought herself long ago accustomed to loss—she had nothing left of her parents. Not even the gold locket that had once held their likenesses. But now she realized how unprepared she had been for anyone to touch this ancient scar.

Glancing back at Lady Thorpe, she tried for a light, careless voice that masked the quivering confusion inside her. "You must have mistaken me for—"

Theo's voice cut through her words. "For your mother—of course she did. Now, bid your *aunt* a good day, Mary. Or we shall be here forever." Leaning close, he muttered, "And don't forget I'm Lord Howe, so that gives me rank over you."

He offered up a charming smile and Molly stared at him, utterly baffled, feeling as tattered now as rags in the wind. *What is going on here?* She wanted to shout the words at someone.

Then Lady Thorpe spoke again, her voice frail with age. "You must come visit me soon, Mary. I do insist. Lord Thorpe and I shall be delighted to receive you at Lanton Hall." She smiled at the younger man in the carriage with her. He said nothing, merely inclined his head as if agreeing.

Molly looked from Theo to Lady Thorpe, still tempted to burst out and demand a full explanation. Was everyone now pretending to be someone else? But she caught the warning glance from Theo and bit off her words.

Lady Thorpe seemed not to notice any of the tension now swirling around the carriage—neither Theo's impatience, nor Molly's confusion. Her lined faced wrinkled with smiles, then she sat back and told her coachman to drive on, pausing only to wave again to them with a hand encased in white kidskin.

When the carriage had rattled away, Molly turned to Theo, the words bursting out, "And just who is Lord Howe? Or Mary? Or Lady Thorpe for that matter?"

Tucking her hand into the crook of his arm, he started down the lane again, towards Winslow Park. "That, my sweet Sweet, is the eccentric of Halsage—I suppose every neighborhood must boast one. And you may count yourself lucky she didn't keep us longer, pulling other names from her past and pegging them onto us."

Molly bit her lower lip. She had guessed this as the truth already, yet she still did not want to give up that slim, slim hope. Oh, she could be so stupid at times.

"So it was all a mistake? Her thinking she knew me or my mother?"

He glanced at her, blue eyes narrowing. "Mistake? What else could it be?"

She wet her lips and tried for the most careless of tones. "Well, I had thought—that is, I don't really know any of my relatives."

Stopping, he stared at her. "Why in blazes would you want to be related to her? She's a harmless enough lunatic, I suppose, but her family avoids her as much as the rest of the world tries to."

Molly glanced down the lane, to where it curved and the carriage had disappeared. "Oh, the poor woman—to be so alone."

Still holding her hand, he started walking again, his stride long enough that Molly had to quicken her pace to stay with him. "Don't waste your pity on her. She goes about happy as a hen in a corn bin, and it's the rest of us who must endure. That fellow with her—that's her butler. Half the time she takes him for Lord Thorpe. And, as you heard, I'm Howe—I have no idea who in blazes he was. Some ancient beau, I think. Still, I'd rather be him than her nephew, as I used to be—he seems to have been a bit of a prig, for she despised him and his father and forever went about telling me how horrible I'd grow up to be!"

Molly let out a laugh, part relief and part amusement. Now that she knew the poor old lady was quite dotish and had meant no harm she had no reason to feel disappointed. It had been impossible all along that Lady Thorpe had known her mother.

Really, it was.

"What a pleasant thing to live with the past still around you no matter what changes," she said, shifting her thought away from her own past. Far better to have empathy, she told herself, with the old woman rather than pity for herself.

Theo gave a shrug. "Don't know about that. I should far rather have the present." He glanced down at her and smiled. "Particularly such a nice present."

Pleasure warmed her and she allowed it, but then she wondered if she, too, might lose her grasp of reality if she dabbled too long in such fantasy. Such a silly thought. Just because Lady Thorpe turned everyone's identity around, didn't mean she had to, too.

Still, she decided that she had had enough of too quickly raised and dashed expectations for that day. Best not to court any more with daydreams about anything being behind Theo's words just now, other than a young gentleman's idle flirtation.

Think of the fifty pounds he's paying you.

With that in mind, she gave him a saucy smile. "Well, ducks, for the present I'm fair famished. What say we toddle back and see about a little something?"

"I could think of a very improper something."

Remembering Sallie's advice, she propped a hand on her hip. "Well, I don't know as you could afford my price for that."

His grin widened. "Perhaps. But I have a feeling you

might be worth going well into hock for—my sweet
Sweet. However, for now let us find something else to satisfy you, eh?"

After strolling back to Winslow Park, Theo had tea
brought for Molly. Then he took her off to the billiards
room, declaring there could be no better way to spend
the remainder of the day.

Stripping off his coat, he had settled to the game with
dedicated concentration, and while Molly had regarded
him with caution at first, there had been nothing lover-
like about his attentions that afternoon. She had
stiffened as he reached around her to show her how to
hold her billiard cue. But while his hands on her arms
lifted her pulse, he seemed not to notice anything but
the balls on the table and the aim of getting one of them
into the net pockets.

Billiards, it seemed, required complete absorption,
and Molly soon found herself as caught up in the art of
calculating angles and her aim. It was only as the light
began to fade that she realized they had played well past
the usual early country hours for dinner.

After racking the cues again, Theo dragged on his
coat, saying, "We might as well go on shocking Simpson
by not changing for dinner."

She found herself unable to resist the glimmer of mischief in his eyes and so she agreed, but Simpson, it
seemed, had determined either to ignore any further
lapses in decorum or at least to offer no reaction to them.
He bowed them into the dining room without comment
as to their attire or to the delayed hour of the meal.

Two footmen immediately brought dishes. Glancing
at them, Molly saw the signs that the cook had had to
struggle to keep them warm. The haddock had been
covered with a sauce that did not quite hide its over-

cooked dryness. Burnt edges scarred a pie. And no sauce could disguise that a dish of French beans had become limp strands.

Distressed that their carelessness with time had been the cause of this disaster, Molly glanced at Simpson. "Gracious, the poor cook! Please do send apologies for having to wait on us."

That drew a shocked stare from him. Glancing around, Molly realized that Theo, too, as well as the footmen were all looking at her with similar dumbfounded expressions.

She realized then that she had spoken quite out of character for a hard-hearted jade and so she added, her accent laid on thick, "Now, what say we tuck in to a good feed!"

She seated herself and held up her soup bowl for serving. Simpson's expression returned to pained disapproval, one of the footmen shook his head and Theo's shoulders relaxed.

So much for my thinking I am any sort of actress, Molly told herself. She was not doing very well at keeping up her pretense. And her feelings tangled between the wish that Theo's father might return at once to get this done, and the dragging desire to put off the confrontation that must come from such a meeting even just a little longer.

I really must keep thinking only of the money I am here to earn, she thought. But somehow her fifty pounds kept getting pushed behind everything else.

They played backgammon again that evening, and Theo was in a mood to flirt. He wanted to wager on the outcome of the games, but Molly only shook her head and insisted, "It wouldn't be right for me to fleece you."

That put him on his mettle and he actually won one of the games, which put him in a good enough mood that he promised to show her the ruins of an old Norman tower which lay near the village of Halsage.

The next day, however, started with clouds thick across

the sky and looking ready for a summer storm. Not wanting to get caught in the rain, Molly declined the offer of a tour of the local ruins.

"A little wetting won't hurt," Theo insisted.

"It wouldn't help, either, for I'm not like to grow from it," she shot back.

He gave a laugh. "Oh, very well. Then what shall we do? Billiards or backgammon? Or shall we take up cards?"

She opted for billiards, thinking that would provide him enough activity for he seemed bursting with energy. But he paced the room and fussed with his own cue and hers so much that finally she said, "Why do you not at least go riding? I've a bit of stitching to do, anyway."

He lifted one dark eyebrow. "First cooking, now sewing—how domestic you sound."

She blushed, but met the glinting humor in his eyes with an unflustered stare. "And why shouldn't I be? I'm a working girl, I am—and I'm not used to this lounging about all day."

With a grin, he came around the billiards table to stand close enough beside her that she could see the darker flecks of cobalt in his blue eyes.

"You won't go outside with me, but you're willing for me to get a wetting. What about my devoted appearance to you? I can't very well go off and leave your side, now can I?"

Leaning his cue against the side of the green baize-covered table, he took up her hand, his fingers playing idly with hers. "'Course, I could think of other ways we could amuse ourselves—ways that would nicely show the staff just how utterly enslaved I am by your charms."

He lifted her hand to brush his lips across the back of it.

Her stomach tightened, but she fixed her smile. She didn't dare reveal how his words and his touch acted on her. It might only serve to encourage him to do more—

and she was starting to see that having high morals was a good deal easier without any temptation to challenge them.

"Enslaved are you?" she said.

"Utterly! Bewitched . . . intoxicated . . . I am yours to command. Or at least I am for as long as we must keep up a good show for everyone." He grinned at her.

"Well, then, perhaps you ought to go out." Tugging her hand away, she held it up before him. "After all, I've no ring yet, now have I? And if you went out and came back with a proper bauble for me, that would set everyone to talking some."

The black eyebrows flattened and a hard look came into his eyes. "Something for you to keep, d'you mean?"

Bracing a hand on her hip, she stared back at him. "I've done nothing but keep to our agreement, ducks, and here you're ready to think me digging for more!"

He stared back at her a moment, then a reluctant smile twisted up the corner of his mouth. "I suppose it would look more as if you were out to bleed me dry if I had some vulgar and expensive trinket for you."

With a grin, he leaned forward to drop a kiss on her cheek. She stepped back at once, but not before his lips had brushed her skin.

Then, eyes alight and with a smile that set her heart soaring, he winked at her. "Blazes, but it was the luckiest day I've ever had when I laid eyes on you. After I stop in Halsage to show off my gift for you, we'll have the entire district talking of this."

He strode from the room, whistling a tune, his hands tucked into his breeches pockets.

She stared after him, her pulse skittering in a very unprofessional manner. Then her hand went up to her cheek. Gracious, but that man could tempt a soul to folly. For a giddy moment, she thought of calling him

back—and of letting him kiss her before she sent him
out. Just a proper kiss. Right on the mouth.

Only that wouldn't be all he wants from you, now would it?
She let out a sigh.

She had seen the heartache Sallie's girls went through
when they allowed their hearts to tangle with what ought
to be just business.

"I'm a woman for hire," she told herself, muttering
the words so that she might remember them. And that
touch of his lips across her skin had meant as little to
him as his comment about being lucky to have met her.

But, oh, how she wanted to see more in it.

Theo had to ride to Taunton for a ring. He thought of
going to Bath—a bit of a ride, that, but there would be a
better selection. However, he had no knowledge of the
shops there, and he and his family were well enough
known in Taunton that he would be able to acquire a
ring from Smyth and Garson Jewelers without having to
do more than pledge the payment.

The selection was simple enough—he asked for the
largest diamond they had. But then a square cut emerald caught his eye and nothing would do but to have it
for Molly. It actually seemed too elegant a ring for his
purposes, set in old, deep-yellow gold with no more than
a small diamond at each side and the emerald glinting
blue flickers in its center. But he could see the stone on
her hand, matching the green of her eyes, so he took it,
and offset such a tasteful choice with a bracelet of diamonds large enough to choke a horse.

The final cost nearly had him choking, but he swallowed back his shock, told himself to remember that he
planned to return the gems after they'd done their work
and he left the shop with velvet pouches heavy in the tail
pockets of his coat.

Blazes, but his father would have a fit at the expense of such stones. He grinned, then started to whistle the tune for "Upon a Summer's Day," but his stride slowed and the song died on his lips. Perhaps, instead of the bracelet and ring, he ought to have adorned Molly with something of his mother's? Only he could not think where his father might have put her jewels—could not even recall seeing them.

And then an image of her flashed before him—dark hair and warm brown eyes, a sweet smile and a round, soft face, and pearls about her neck and dangling from her ears.

She had always worn pearls.

What an odd thing to recollect.

And, for some reason, it cast a darker shadow over the day than did the clouds overhead. He tried to shake off the sudden downhearted turn in his mood, but it persisted as he rode back along the road from Taunton. Blazes, why should some stray memory bring on this sense of . . . of what? It wasn't as if he had ever missed his mother really. He had hardly known her. But perhaps that was what made him shift in the saddle now, uneasy in his skin.

It was just this not being certain of anything, he told himself. He had never been a patient sort, and having to cool his heels, waiting for his father, did not set well with him. True enough, Molly was proving a good enough companion, but it would be far better to be at home, sporting with her in bed than all this riding about. After all, he might not have much more time with her.

His frown deepened at that.

There would still be plenty of time after this other matter was settled.

The village of Halsage came up before him as fat rain drops began to splatter into the dust of the road. Pulling his hat lower, he turned his gelding for the sign of The

Four Feathers to share a pint and the sight of the jewels he had for his 'intended.'

And if that doesn't start gossip that'll reach my father and bring him home, nothing will, he decided, his jaw set. But he kept thinking that perhaps it would not be such a bad thing if his father took just a few more days to return.

Molly tried to settle to sewing. She had two more dresses to hem—an orange one for evening and the bright peacock blue. Neither of them colors a lady really ought to wear, she supposed, but Molly liked how they caught the eye. She would keep them all when she returned to London, though most seemed far too fine for venturing to the fish market at Billingsgate, or the fruit and vegetable stalls of Covent Garden. Perhaps having them would tempt her beyond her usual round of shops. She could always take Sundays off if she wanted, for that day they usually ate what was left from Saturday.

She found, however, that today she had no patience to set an even line of stitches. After no more than one hem basted, she set it aside and went to the window.

The clouds had thickened and darkened, but despite her reluctance for a wetting, she knew she might also not have such an opportunity again. Theo's father might return this very afternoon. Or when Theo came back, he would want her attention—he was, after all, paying for her time. So she made up her mind.

It was not as if she had not been invited, after all.

And she simply had to know completely, utterly, and for a certainty that there was no chance.

After exchanging slippers for sturdy half-boots, tucking her curls into a brown and white "drum" hat trimmed with blue, and digging out her much-worn pair of kid gloves, she went downstairs. She paused only to ask a footman for the use of an umbrella and the direction for Lanton Hall.

That earned her a look brimming with curiosity, but the fellow seemed far too well-trained to ask any questions, and so she set out with a black umbrella tucked under her arm.

The footman had offered simple enough directions—through the woods to the east along the footpath, and then a left just after a footbridge across the stream. But somehow she did not find the stream. She did, however, find her way back to the lane where she and Theo had met Lady Thorpe the other day, and there she stood, unable to decide which way to go.

London streets, she decided, were far easier to navigate.

As she hesitated, impatient and wondering if she ought to go back to Winslow Park, a fox trotted out from the apple trees on the opposite side of the lane.

Or rather, it bobbed out, and she thought that it must be injured. Then she realized it had only one foreleg. It stopped at once in the lane, quite steady on its three legs. Wide, dark eyes regarded her without wariness from a pointed face that was not unlike a dog's face.

"Gracious, this must be where odd things happen," Molly said, muttering to herself.

She stared back at the fox, a little wary. Tales about the tigers of India had been enough to give her a healthy respect for wild beasts. However, she knew very little about foxes. She had only seen colored prints of them in childhood story books, with their distinctive red bodies and black-masked faces. She did know, however, that they were supposed to be timid creatures.

Only this one seemed not to have read that particular childhood book, for it stared back as bold as if it owned this land.

Then one black ear—tall and pointed—swiveled, and the black, pointed face swung around as the fox glanced back from where it had come. A moment later a girl popped out from the woods and into the lane and stopped still.

And Molly decided this spot indeed had to be the one place in Somerset where all odd things happened.

Eight

Not a girl, Molly decided after a second glance. A young lady. A rather plain one who seemed more fey than human.

Short, reddish-gold hair curled about a pointed face— one that reminded Molly strongly of the fox's face. Only instead of brown eyes, wide, blue-green eyes stared at Molly from under arched, sandy-hued eyebrows. The girl had a straight, wide mouth and an even straighter nose. Mud stained the hem of her faded blue gown, giving her the look of a street urchin. A twig stuck out of her hair. She wore neither gloves nor bonnet nor even a shawl, and the summer sun had browned the bare arms that showed from the short sleeves of her high-waisted gown.

No wonder she had seemed a girl at first glance, for she was as slim as one and as untidy. But now Molly noticed that though she might be slender, small, high breasts filled out her gown, and though her face was unlined, a rather serious maturity lay in her eyes.

However, she had to be the least intimidating person Molly had ever met.

Hoping to put the girl at ease, Molly smiled, then said, "Hello. You don't happen to know the way to Lanton Hall, do you?"

The girl's chin dropped and she gave Molly back a measuring stare. When she did not answer, Molly began to wonder if she would not because she had guessed

Molly's identity and had been told not to associate with a woman of her reputation, or perhaps she could not.

Finally, the girl said, her voice pitched so soft that Molly found herself leaning forward in order to hear, "You must be Theo's mistress."

Molly blinked at such a blunt statement, but the young lady tipped her head to the side and added, "Oh, don't worry. It doesn't put me out if you are. My sister never would have been happy with him."

Mouth falling open, Molly stared at this odd young lady. So Theo had had an interest in her sister? Only somehow it had not gone anywhere. Had he made promises to this girl's sister and broken them? Frowning now, she asked, "Do you mean to say he was to wed your sister?"

The girl shook her head. "Not exactly. But if Theo didn't tell you about it, I suppose I should not, either. Good day."

She turned to start back into the woods, giving a low whistle to the fox, but Molly stepped forward, "Wait! I mean, please—that is, Lord, ducks, but you can't go poppin' in and out like this, leaving me half lost."

In more ways than one, Molly thought, her mind still turning with questions about the hints this young lady had dropped. She ought to have realized that a gentleman as attractive as Theo would be bound to have more than a few ladies interested. But what had happened between them? Was their parting due to Theo's faults? Or to the lady? He didn't seem particularly heart-broken, but then he also seemed very likely to put a smile over any pain—just out of stubbornness, if nothing else.

The girl paused, the fox now pressed close to the muddy hem of her gown. "I beg your pardon. My sisters are threatening a London Season if I don't learn a few manners, so. . . ."

Turning, she spread her skirts and dropped a pretty

curtsy, then said with precise formality, "I am Miss Sylvain Harwood—how do you do?"

Molly stared back, uncertain whether to reply in keeping with her pretense or to obey the urge to follow the good manners trained into her during her youngest years. Sylvain seemed to mistake her hesitation for ignorance, for she leaned forward and confided, "You're supposed to curtsy back and say your name and that it's a pleasure. You don't actually have to tell me how you do. It's stupid to ask questions you don't want answered, but so is most of being polite."

Fighting down a smile, Molly agreed with this, then dropped a quick curtsy and said, "I'm Molly Sweet."

Sylvain nodded. "I know. Mrs. Brown's cousin is the upstairs maid at Harwood."

"Mrs. Brown?" Molly asked.

"The cook at Winslow Park. Oh, and I should introduce Trace. His name is actually a play on the Spanish for three. Terrance named him. But he can't offer you his paw because he lost one in a trap—Trace, that is, not Terrance. If he likes you, you may pet him."

With a dubious glance at the fox, Molly decided she would probably offend if she declined such an offer. Bending down, she stretched out a hand. The fox hesitated but Sylvain gave him a nudge with her leg. After a brief glance at his mistress, the fox bobbed toward Molly on his three legs.

Eyes watchful, Molly kept still. The fox returned her look with just as much caution. Two feet away the creature paused, sniffed the air, then edged forward, looking ready to run if Molly dared so much as to let go her breath. Whiskers lightly tickled her fingertips, and then he allowed her the barest touch of his head. He had surprisingly wiry fur.

As she straightened, the fox turned and bobbed back

to Sylvain, glancing over his shoulder, his dark eyes less wary and now filled with shy interest.

Sylvain seemed to approve of the exchange for she smiled. That changed everything. Her eyes brightened, and the smile added an elfin charm to her face, curving the straight lips into an attractive bow. Her features no longer looked so severe, nor so awkward.

Gracious, if she left off the muddy dresses and the twigs in her hair, she would quite catch the eye.

The young woman seemed to have no idea of her charm, however, and she merely said, as if bestowing an honor, "Trace likes you."

The fox had sat down next to Sylvain and now opened his mouth to pant, revealing a pink tongue and a gleam of sharp teeth. Molly would not have been so interested in having him sniff her fingers if she had first glimpsed those teeth. They were not as long as those she had seen on the tiger heads that had adorned some of the officer's quarters in India, but they looked capable of taking off a finger with one snap.

"We can walk with you to Lanton—it's not far," Sylvain offered.

"Thank you," Molly said, coming forward. But what she really wanted to ask was more about Theo and Sylvain's sister. *Only it's nothing to do with me and I ought to just mind my own business.* And still the words popped right out, "So why did Theo not marry your sister?"

Sylvain seemed not to mind her prying, but started into the woods, taking the footpath that had brought Molly to the lane.

"Oh, she married someone else instead. I rather thought she wanted Theo, but she changed her mind, which is just like Cecila. She was even going to be Lady Nevin for a bit, but now she's Mrs. Dawes of London and Penelope—she's my other sister—is Lady Nevin."

Pausing, Sylvain glanced over her shoulder with a

frown. "I suppose that all sounds terribly ramshackle, doesn't it?"

It did. But Molly found relief slipping through her that Sylvain's sister had been the flighty one. So she only shook her head and said, "I'm not in much of a spot to judge others overmuch."

Sylvain started forward again. "That's sounds wise. I hate to be judged—and I always am. All I am supposed to know, or care about, are pretty dresses and dancing and dull things like sewing and household economies!"

Molly smiled. The girl made these sound fates worse than death. "That doesn't sound too awful."

"It is if you do not like dancing, or sewing, or having to put on gowns that you will only tear the hem on." She slanted a glance back at Molly. "Do you know Terrance as well as Theo?"

Again, Molly shook her head, and then she had to step over the roots of a towering tree—oh, how she wished they could at least have walked upon the dirt lane. Even the cobbles of London were seeming so much easier on the feet than this rambling, uneven path. "No, I've not met Theo's brother. I only just met Theo at a . . . at Mrs. Ellis's house."

Sylvain slid her a glance again, then asked, "Are you actually going to marry Theo?"

Putting her gaze on the ground, Molly focused on avoiding yet more roots. She supposed that if she could ask Sylvain straight out about her sister's past with Theo, there was no reason the girl could not ask about her future with him. Only there wasn't one to discuss.

Preferring to stay as honest as she could, she said, "You might say it depends on what his father thinks."

"Really? And you don't mind that Theo . . . well, that he visits the sort of places where he met you? Terrance does that, too—I'm not supposed to know about any of it, but everyone in Halsage knows about the Winslows."

"Do they? What do they know?"

"That they are shockingly wild. At least Terrance is, and Theo seems to mean to follow him. Do you mind? Cecila did—which is why I think she and Theo quarreled so much. It always seemed to be over him—well, his being some place she did not like him to be."

"Well, any man I marry won't be needing a place such as where we met—I'd make sure of it!" And she would, too, Molly thought. She had made up her mind about that some time ago, after enough chats with Sallie's girls to have an idea of just what brought a man to Sallie's and what it took to keep his interest there.

It had surprised her that most of the girls had their regulars, and that the gentleman themselves seemed to prefer an established arrangement. But Sallie had always said, "They're creatures of habit. It takes treatin' 'em bad enough that they'll look for new, more pleasant habits to get into. So you just have to make certain the habits you set with 'em are too enjoyable to leave."

As Sylvain stepped from the woods and into open land, she stopped and turned to Molly, a puzzled frown tightening her sandy brows. "But just how do you make certain he would never need such a place?"

And oh, don't I just talk too much, Molly thought, biting her lower lip. Perhaps that was why young ladies weren't supposed to talk to women such as she was supposed to be—it wasn't only to shelter the young ladies, it also kept worldly women such as she was pretending to be from getting backed into corners.

Well, she had to say something. The girl looked quite stubborn enough to out wait Methuselah for an answer. Only what could she say that wouldn't lead to more questions?

Taking a breath, Molly tried to think of what Sallie might reply. "Look at it this way, ducks—a fellow's always going to look. He can't help that. But if he's got what he wants already in hand, why spend his time and money and effort for anything else?"

Head tilting to the side, Sylvain seemed to think this over. Before she could ask for elaboration—which she certainly ought not to know, and which Molly feared she wouldn't be able to provide—Molly glanced across the open land toward the square house of gray stone that stood on a small rise of land.

"Ah, and there's Lanton Hall. Thanks ever so much. I don't want to keep you, and I'll stay to the lanes goin' back."

The change of topic distracted Sylvain well enough. She glanced at the house, then at the darkening sky and gave a sigh. "I suppose I should go home as well. I am already late out. Oh, if Lady Thorpe offers cakes, take the almond—they're wonderfully sweet."

Molly paused, her interest caught. "Really? What sort of almonds does she use?"

Sylvain gave a shrug. "I just eat them. I suppose though that I ought to warn you she is a bit odd. But I like her. She's not one of those who think I have to talk lots just to prove I'm not really shy."

Molly gave a laugh. "Ducks, you're one of the least shy people I've ever met."

"Of course I'm not." With a smile, she thrust out her hand and with a firm grip she shook Molly's hand, almost more like a man. "I am glad we met. I like you. And I hope you do marry Theo. You'd be good for him."

With that, she turned, gave a whistle to her fox and disappeared into the woods.

Molly stared after her a moment, bemused by the girl's opinion of her value to Theo—not one that any would share. A penniless orphan with no family, no assets, and only a history of working in a brothel good for a young gentleman? Not likely. But it showed what a good heart the girl had. And how innocent she was. And

Molly suspected that if the girl were given the chance she might well adopt Molly, much as it seemed she had that three-legged fox.

And if the gossip had already spread about her, she could imagine that the looks she'd get from the residents of Halsage would make those she had been earning at Winslow Park seem positively welcoming.

A drop of wetness splashed onto her cheek. She glanced up at the clouds, then opened her umbrella and hurried toward Lanton Hall.

Thankfully, she reached the graveled drive before the rain began to fall in earnest. Droplets still managed to stain her skirts, blown sideways by the wind. But she gained the gray stone steps to the entrance and soon stood under the front portico. Applying the iron knocker to the door, she waited only a moment and then the young man who had been with Lady Thorpe yesterday opened the door.

Stomach churning at her own audacity in arriving uninvited, Molly pushed back her shoulders. "I'm here to see Lady Thorpe."

He glanced at her, then stepped back, allowing her inside.

Lowering her umbrella, she came in. Roses—pink ones, white ones, yellow, red, dark golden ones, some striped, some merely buds, some full blown, some with masses of petals and some with single rows—decorated every table in the hall, adding a perfumed scent. Molly glanced around, taking in the colors and the smells, and then she found herself facing Lady Thorpe's butler again.

"I'm—" she started, but he cut off her words at once.

"Miss Sweet," he finished for her, disapproval tight in his tone. "I don't know what you're game is with the Winslows, but her ladyship's care is my look out. And I won't have no London lightskirt taking advantage of her."

Molly stiffened. "My, but the gossip has been busy."

"I made it a point to ask after you. Whatever rig you're running with the Winslows, that's their look out. But just because her mind wanders a bit, that don't mean her ladyship is ripe for your plucking."

Face hot now, Molly regarded the young man. He had an honest, round face. Dark blond hair was brushed back and worn short, and his gray eyes looked as dark as the clouds outside. Dressed in black with a yellow waistcoat, he was not tall—Molly could look him straight in the eye. But he had a sturdy look to him, as if he could easily pick her up and put her from the house if she would not leave on her own.

Chin lifting, she returned his stare, her pride hurting. "I came to visit an old woman who thought she knew my mother—that's the only rig I have. And if you think I. . . ."

Before she could go on, Lady Thorpe's fragile voice drifted into the hall, sounding distressed, "Grieg, I cannot find Captain Villars anywhere—not even under my bed!"

Both Molly and Lady Thorpe's butler, Grieg, turned as her ladyship came down the blue-carpeted stairs at the back of the hall. Her ladyship paused on the upper landing, then squinted into the hall before coming down the stairs. "Oh, dear—a guest. Do forgive me, but I have lost my cat. Grieg, can you please find Captain Villars? Oh, but I suppose first you must bring some refreshments for . . . for. . . ."

Her words trailed off as she approached.

Molly picked up her courage and held out her hand. "It's Miss Sweet, your ladyship. We met yesterday."

That pulled an even more distressed look from the older woman. "Did we?"

Molly shot a glance at the butler and found him scowling at her, but she was determined to show him she did not mean any harm to Lady Thorpe. She turned back to that tiny slip of a lady. "I shouldn't expect you to remember me. It was only the briefest meeting. On the lane between here and Winslow Park—I'm staying with the Winslows."

Lady Thorpe's faded eyes brightened. "Are you? And how is dear Lady Winslow and her little boys? Such rascals they are—always into mischief."

Molly's smile stiffened, but she caught the warning shake of Grieg's head and so she said nothing. She did not have to. Lady Thorpe had again turned to her butler, "Grieg, do bring refreshment into the drawing room." She then tucked a trembling, age-withered hand into the crook of Molly's arm. "This way, dear Miss—what did you say your name was again?"

"Sweet, my lady."

"Ah, yes . . . like Sweet William—I must remember that."

She started toward a side door, but Grieg stepped forward at once. "This way, my lady, to the drawing room." He shot another frown at Molly and then started up the stairs, glancing back as if to make certain that her ladyship followed.

Molly kept her steps slow to match Lady Thorpe's tottering pace.

On the upper floor, Grieg led the way to a pretty, yellow painted room that overlooked the front of the house. Even though it was summer, a fire crackled in the hearth, and it was welcome enough, for the storm had chilled the day.

As Lady Thorpe moved to a chair, Molly started to undo the ribbons of her bonnet, but Grieg leaned closer and muttered, "You won't be staying that long."

She shot him a hard look. While she admired the protection he gave his mistress, it had started to irritate.

Defiantly, she took off her bonnet, then tugged off her gloves. Handing both to him, she said, "Thanks, but I think that'll be all I need of you."

She could almost swear she heard his teeth grinding, but as Lady Thorpe was again asking him to bring refreshments, he bowed, shot a warning glance at Molly and left.

Easing herself into a gold satin brocade covered chair near the fire, Lady Thorpe gestured toward the chair opposite. "Do sit down, Miss . . . Miss. . . ?"

"I wish you'd call me Molly—or Mary, as you did yesterday," Molly said, coming forward and hoping to stir Lady Thorpe's memory.

Her ladyship gazed back, the wrinkles on her brow creased and her eyes worried. Then her face relaxed and she smiled. "Do let me ring for refreshments. Oh, but where did I put that bell?"

Over the next three-quarters of an hour, Molly kept thinking of Theo's words—that it was not Lady Thorpe who suffered from her lack of memory. He had the right of it. Molly endured with a stiff smile as her ladyship kept forgetting who she was and why she was here. When Grieg returned with a footman and a silver tea set, the butler remained positioned just behind Lady Thorpe with a stern stare locked on Molly.

As if he's expecting me to steal a spoon, Molly thought, her patience worn to the nub.

Only once, after pouring tea, did Lady Thorpe's eyes sharpen. She stared at Molly then, and said, "My, but you look so like Amy—only Amy's been dead for years."

Then she went off, talking about her cats, and Molly soon learned that while Captain Villars was a cat she wasn't sure if he could not be found because he had run off or because he, too, had passed on years ago.

She could not really make conversation—not when she had to keep starting and restarting the same topics. And she could not get Lady Thorpe to fix on the past long enough to determine if there was the least connection between them.

An unlikely thing, really, but Molly had had to make the effort at least.

Only she ought to have listened to Theo's caution that everyone did their best to avoid the old lady.

Still, she could not help but want to be patient as she could with her ladyship. Grand as she and her house were, what a terrible fate to be left with a rambling mind and only cats for company. One of them—a great, orange cat—came strolling in during tea and sat on the edge of the rug, washing his paw and his face as if that was the most important task in the world.

She had some consolation, however, in the food. Lady Thorpe had a gem of a cook. There were dainty apricot tarts, thin slices of plum cake, and macaroons so tempting that Molly almost ate all of them. The almond cakes that Sylvain had noted Molly did give into, eating every one, and telling herself that it wasn't so bad, for they were quite small.

Finally, with her appetite satisfied, even if nothing else was, Molly admitted defeat and rose. "I shouldn't take up any more of your ladyship's time."

"But you only just arrived. Do allow me to at least ring for refreshments. Oh, but the tea is here already." Lady Thorpe glanced at the silver tea service, her expression surprised, and Molly decided she really must leave. It seemed as much a strain for her ladyship to be dealing with her as it was for her to deal with Lady Thorpe's forgetfulness.

Her decision seemed to please Grieg, for he left at once and came back with her hat, gloves, and umbrella.

Lady Thorpe smiled and came forward. "It has been lovely, Miss . . . Miss Swenton was it not?"

"Sweet," Molly said, the correction by now automatic. "Thank you for seeing me."

"You must promise me to come again—only not on Thursday. Lord Thorpe prefers me to have one day a week when I do not take callers. He says it tires me too much."

Molly wasn't certain if this instruction really came

from her butler or her late husband. In either case, it was perhaps a wise idea. At the moment, Lady Thorpe looked as fragile as crystal, as if she might shatter if knocked too hard.

"Thank you, but I won't be stopping long in the neighborhood."

Lady Thorpe's smile faded. "Oh? What a pity. Well, promise me to call again if you do stay. Will you do that?"

It seemed a safe enough promise, though Molly still felt a twinge at giving it. She was already pretending to be something she was not, and that seemed quite a large enough sin on her soul, even if she was doing it for good reasons.

Still, what odds she'd be here much longer?

With that in mind, she offered up as good a curtsy as she knew and then followed Grieg downstairs to the front door with her ladyship holding her arm.

She was glad of Lady Thorpe's company, though she gave the older woman more support than the other way around. However, it kept Grieg from dropping any more hints about how unwelcome she was.

But as he opened the front door, Lady Thorpe glanced out at the slanting rain and then turned to Molly. "My dear, where is your carriage? Grieg, did you not send for it?"

"I walked, my lady."

"Well, you cannot walk out in this wet. Grieg, have my coach brought to take Miss Street home."

Molly tried to protest. Grieg, too, looked unhappy but he moved at once to obey—most likely thinking that the sooner he had Molly away, the better, even if it was in her ladyship's coach. And Molly could only hope that while he was gone, her ladyship didn't wander off.

That did not happen, though there was a near miss when an elegant gray cat with a feather-plume of a tail strode into the hall and her ladyship brightened, saying, "Ah, Captain Villars, there you are."

The cat glanced at Molly, froze in place, yellow eyes enormous, then turned and ran—obviously skittish with strangers. Lady Thorpe started after the cat, but as Molly had a vision of her getting utterly lost in her own house, she caught her ladyship's elbow before she got far and diverted her attention by asking if she grew all these roses.

Amazingly, Lady Thorpe could name the type of every rose—though Molly had no idea if she was naming them correctly.

"Lord Thorpe and I planted them when we first married and moved here—it was my one consolation from being so cut off from my family," Lady Thorpe said, touching a pink-tipped white rose. "They did not approve of Lord Thorpe, you see. Of course, they never approved of poor Amy's husband either. So dreadfully high in the instep, my family. It had to be money and a title, or they wanted nothing to do with any man for us!"

Molly's pulse quickened. "Was your sister named Amy—or was she only called that as a shortening for Amelia?"

Lady Thorpe frowned at the question, her eyes alert. Before she could answer, Grieg arrived to announce that the carriage was ready and Molly had to take her leave.

With an inward sigh, she told herself it was for the best. She was grasping for straws, and when she ended with a handful of hay she'd only be disappointed.

So she put on a bright smile. She really ought to be grateful for her ladyship's hospitality. And that she had her own mind sharp—there were some things that perhaps money and a title and a lovely home didn't make up for.

"Do tell your cook that those almond cakes are quite the best I've ever had," she said, taking hold of the old lady's trembling hand.

Lady Thorpe's dull eyes brightened and she straightened a little. "How nice. Shall I have Mrs. Herbert write out her recipe for you?"

It was too much temptation—the almond cakes had been morsels of sweetness with hints of lemon and orange mixed in. She ought to go, what with Grieg now frowning at her and the horses standing outside in the rain, and the coachman waiting. But she accepted Lady Thorpe's offer.

Grieg sent a footman to the kitchen with the request, and he must have told the fellow to be quick about it, for the footman returned in what seemed an instant with a hastily penciled list of ingredients. Folding up the paper, Molly again said good-bye and was soon seated inside Lady Thorpe's carriage.

It kept her dry, but it also smelled of bitter apples which must have been used to keep the moths from the velvet upholstery—and which had only partially succeeded. Creaking and swaying, the coach made its lumbering way to Winslow Park, and Molly thought she would never risk taking such an ancient vehicle farther.

After thanking the coachman, she ran up the steps of Winslow Park, her umbrella open overhead and held tight against the gusting wind.

With a sigh of relief, she pushed open the heavy front door and let herself into the house.

Then she stood on the doorstep, dripping umbrella in one hand and her face reddening under the gaze of three startled dogs and two disapproving gentleman.

Simpson she knew, but she did not at once recognize the older gentleman with him, and then she blinked in shock.

Eyes as blue as Theo's—only a touch more bloodshot—stared at her, and she could only imagine that this must be Squire Winslow come home.

Nine

With a discreet half-bow, Simpson edged himself from the hall, taking with him the squire's dripping hat and greatcoat. Molly wished she could go with him. She had come to Winslow Park to be introduced to the squire, only she had not been ready for it to happen just now. Where in . . . in blazes was Theo? This was his plan, his family, and he was the one who was supposed to bear the wrath of this rather daunting gentleman.

It was not that he was a large man—Theo stood at least a half foot taller. Stocky, with legs that looked bowed from decades spent on horseback, he seemed a harsh man. Hard with himself and others, she judged by how his mouth dragged down at the corners. He dressed in somber black—riding boots, breeches, high-collared coat and waistcoat, with only a touch of white showing in his plain cravat and shirt and in the shock of thick, silver-white hair which he wore long enough that the ends curled around heavy jowls.

In contrast to that silver hair, thick black eyebrows rode tight together over those sharp blue eyes. His cheeks and nose shown ruddy; she judged the glow came from drink for even with the storm, the air was not chill enough.

One of the dogs—a shaggy black and white with floppy ears—offered a growl, and the squire silenced it with a look and snap of his fingers. The dog glanced at the squire and stopped its noise. But the squire kept his gaze on her, staring at her as if taking her measure as he tapped a hunting whip against his boots.

She rather wished he did not have that whip. But Theo had insisted his father would not resort to physical violence. And if he wanted her driven out, he could set his dogs on her.

The dogs gathered close to the squire, the black and white one still looking as if he would enjoy chasing her from the house, but the reddish-coated one gave a tentative wag of his tail, and the third—a mix of brown and white—gave a tremendous yawn and sat down. All of them had soaked, dripping hair, muddy paws, and smelled of wet dog.

Shaking out her umbrella, she pulled it closed and waited. Best to let the squire make the first move. Rather like a game of backgammon where it helped to first gauge another's skills and weaknesses.

He continued to stare at her. A clock ticked away the seconds, almost as loud as her pounding heart.

Then one black eyebrow arched in a gesture she recognized from Theo, and he said, his voice roughened from years of drink, "Not much size to you, is there?"

Lifting her chin, she stared back. A bit of a bully, she judged, to attack her in that fashion. She knew better than to show any weakness.

With one hand on her hip and bracing the other on her umbrella, she slipped into her best Sallie accent. "Don't know about that, ducks, but I'd say there's certainly more than enough of you."

She allowed her stare to fix on his portly belly. Then she looked up at his face again with a challenge.

Eyes glimmering, his scowl darkened, but then he threw back his head and gave a laugh. The dogs all stood, their tails wagging. The squire ignored them. Sobering, he stared at her.

What in perdition had Theo been thinking to bring

home such a brazen wench? Oh, she was toothsome enough, as any man could see. But, by gads, this was a respectable house. Had been for generations.

Had the boy been foxed? If so, he ought to have come to his senses when he sobered and taken the girl away.

Simpson had been muttering on about something to do with the wench, only he hadn't been attending. He'd ridden hard through the night and what he wanted were dry clothes, a thick sirloin, and his pipe. His bad ankle ached from the wet, his back tooth hurt and his trip to Suffolk had been a waste for Sir Charles would not come to terms on a price for that mare.

Gads, but what a plague. She'd had just the bloodlines he'd wanted. Out of Young Giantess by the underrated Diomed, who came by Sorcerer from the great Matchem himself. A mare certain to produce a Derby winner if ever. But he'd not go a shilling over a thousand for her—by gads, he would not. No, he had been taken once, spending too much for a brute of a stallion that he had been lucky to sell off. He would not be gulled a second time.

It rankled, of course, that that stallion now looked to have mended his ways. But if he found the right mare to breed to him, he'd still come off best where it mattered.

Thinking now on that, he eased his weight from his bad leg—broken on a hunt years ago—and he glared at the wench. Caesar nudged his hand for a pet, and that reminded him, too, that he had the dogs to see dried and fed.

He did not want to be dealing with shipping off his son's mistress just now—no matter how round a figure she sported. Gads, had Theo left her here just for him to deal with? It would be like the lad to be just so careless. Damn, but he would have a talk with him about this. Time he grew up a bit, now that Terrance. . . .

The squire cut off that thought, and frowned even more at this pert strumpet. He did not want to be thinking of his eldest—no, he corrected himself. He had only one son now.

"Not much size, eh, but plenty of sauce. Only it won't do for Theo to have his fancy piece here. Simpson's packing your things to send you back to wherever he found you."

"I'm not his fancy piece. I'm Miss Molly Sweet, and I'm—"

"She's my bride."

Molly swung around, and the squire turned his attention from her to his son, who had stepped in through the open front door, rain dripping from his hat and darkening his coat and breeches. The dogs bounded forward at once to greet him with barks and whines, and Theo absently stroked wet heads as he slanted Molly a hint of a smile.

Letting out a breath, she stepped aside as he came in and then shut the front door behind him.

Father and son faced each other, and Molly watched. Like her, the dogs settled down, almost as if they, too, sensed the tension gathering. The scene, Molly thought, had the same compelling fascination of two carriages bowling along a London street and about to collide— disaster pending. And which of them, if any, would come out unscathed?

The squire's voice rose first, rumbling into the hall with indignant outrage, "Bride?"

Theo pulled off his hat and tossed it onto a side table. "Yes, bride. And I've just got a ring for you, my sweet Sweet." Fumbling with his coat tail pockets, he pulled out two velvet pouches. The slight agitation in his movements was the only betrayal of his feelings, for his manner otherwise seemed untroubled.

Eyes narrowing, the squire glared at his son. The whip had stopped tapping. "A ring is it?"

With a forced smile, Theo pulled out an emerald and

diamond ring. Molly could not help but gasp, and then the most appalling greed swept through her—gracious, but to have such a thing as her very own. This must indeed be how girls were tempted into making unwise decisions.

But oh, what a fine bit of flash.

Dragging off her glove, she did not have to pretend in order to thrusting out her hand with eager interest. "Coo, ducks—for me?"

The dogs, too, seemed eager to see the gems, though they looked disappointed after a quick sniff of her hand and strolled back to the squire's side.

"Just a trifle, my sweet Sweet. I've a bracelet for you as well." With a grim smile that seemed a parody of his usual one, he put the ring on her finger and then spilled diamonds into his gloved palm.

Molly's eyes bulged. She shot a worried glance at Theo's father—Lord knew, if she were Theo's parent just now, she'd be ready to box his ears for such reckless extravagance.

The squire stood still, his face red as flame, his expression as fixed as that of a stone gargoyle, and Molly glanced at Theo. She had never thought of family as anything but an asset, but now she saw that having relations brought its own difficulties—such as getting along with each other.

These two seemed to be doing their best to do the opposite and antagonize each other.

"There!" Theo said, fastening the bracelet around Molly's wrist. It felt like an iron manacle and weighed almost as much. Still, she put on a smile and held it up to admire how it blazed like a hundred-candle chandelier.

"Coo, ducks. . . ." she said, unable to think what else might be in character. "It fair takes my breath."

"I supposed you've a Special License to wed in your pocket, too," the squire grumbled. The dogs all shifted their gaze to Theo, as if copying the squire's interest.

Theo frowned and hesitated for an instant, and the

squire's eyes narrowed a touch more. An unpleasant sensation swept into Molly that Theo had misjudged his own father—the man looked as canny to her as any vendor in Covent Garden, and perhaps Theo had been mistaken to think he could fool his father about anything.

Still, she was here to play a part—and her fifty pounds depended on this going well. So she straightened and set her hand on her hip again—that seemed as defiant a pose as any.

"Special License! A proper wedding's what he promised me—ain't it, ducks?" she added, throwing him what she hoped appeared to be a beguiling smile.

Theo brightened, turned just enough to slip her a wink and then faced his father again, "That's right. I brought her home so the banns could be called."

Folding his arms, the squire dropped his chin so it almost rested on his chest. "Then you've talked to the vicar, have you?"

"Well . . . not yet. Blazes, we only just got here!"

Molly stepped closer to Theo and tucked her arm into his—his sodden coat smelled of wet wool, but she found a measure of reassurance from his warmth and size. "My Theo's had other things to think of," she said, and then she fluttered her lashes up at him.

For a moment, he glanced down at her, as if distracted, and Molly stared up at him, caught for an instant by the sweep of black lashes against his skin and the depth of blue in his eyes. They were far deeper in color than his father's really.

The squire's voice made her jump, and jerked Theo's stare from her. "Then I'll just go talk to the vicar myself, shall I? You're not the first man to marry his mistress—and gads, while she's not what I'd have picked for you, it's about time one of my . . . it's about time my son gave me grandsons!"

At the squire's tone, the dogs began to pace, restless

and agitated. Theo's face darkened into a scowl, but the squire's mouth twisted up.

Molly shivered. Wasn't the squire supposed to be thundering about, disowning Theo? Why this sudden acceptance of her?

She stared at him, wondering if he had guessed their deception, or if he was merely trying to see if Theo bluffed. Then she glanced at Theo. Would he give in now and admit defeat?

Jaw set, Theo glared at his father. "I can talk to the vicar on my own, thank you!"

The squire's eyes glimmered. "Best do so. It's four weeks to call 'em, so why delay?"

Four weeks! Molly almost uttered the words. But Theo had reached for her hand and gave it a squeeze as the squire turned and stomped up the stairs, his dogs standing to shake the water from their coats before they bounded after their master.

Molly glanced at Theo, her lips parted to ask him what they did now, but he only shook his head. Then he gave her hand a kiss. "I've the vicar to see. We'll talk later, my sweet Sweet."

With that, he picked up his hat and slammed out the front door.

Molly glanced up at the stairs—now empty—then to the front door—now shut. The only movement left in the hall was herself and the puddles.

With a shake of her head, she started up the stairs.

Maybe she had really been blessed all these years not having family. A nice thought, that, but even with all this fuss, not one she could quite bring her heart to accept.

She had no chance to speak to Theo alone before dinner. And the squire and his dogs dined with them, making for strained conversation over the meal.

Stubborn as two pigs in the same holding pen, Molly decided, glancing from one to the other. The squire kept his attention on his food, making a good meal. Occasionally, he tossed scraps from the table to his dogs, addressing his comments to them—Caesar, Marcus, and Plato, though she could not tell which dog wore what name.

Theo ignored the dogs and his father, picking over the items on his plate as if he could not summon any interest in much of anything.

Deciding that a brazen woman would not give tuppence about the subtleties of atmosphere, Molly chattered about the bad weather, praised the dishes set out, and tried to do what she could to make herself seem a bad bargain. She turned over the china to note its maker, tested the crystal for the true ring of lead, and drained her glass every time a footman filled it.

And I might have saved myself the effort for all the notice I'm getting, she thought, as both men continued their silent battle of wills and ignored her.

She had worn the peacock-blue paisley patterned gown, and the bracelet and ring. But she might as well have shown up in her white muslin with flour dusted across it, and with her apron and cook's cap on. Only she wasn't supposed to be a cook, she was supposed to be a harlot.

What she felt like was a stick of furniture. Even the dogs got more attention.

At last the meal ended and she used the excuse of the call of nature to make a hasty exit and take herself to her room. Fifty pounds did not include having to endure any more of this evening, she decided.

After changing her dress for a muslin wrapper and the short chemise that she liked to sleep in, she sat down on her bed to brush out her hair.

Her childhood in India had given her a taste for sleeping in just a linen chemise. While England lacked the heat that had led to such a habit, the custom gave her the comfort of keeping something from that long-ago life. She had also hated the way her legs used to tangle in the ankle-length, itchy woolen nightgown she had been made to wear at St. Marylebone's, when she'd had to sleep with six other girls, usually on nothing more than mats on the floor.

When she had left, her first act of defiance had been to start sleeping in the chemise usually worn during the day under a gown. And to vow she would sleep no more than two to a bed in future.

As she brushed her hair, a quiet rap sounded at the door and then it opened and Theo came into her room.

Sitting up, she started to protested, "Here now, what—!"

Theo put a finger to his lips and glanced out into the darkened hallway.

He had his coat off, replaced by a gold and black dressing gown that swept down to his ankles, but which he had not bothered to button. She glimpsed his buff breeches and white stockings underneath it. His shirt lay open at the neck, and it looked as if he had taken off his waistcoat as well as his cravat.

As usual, his black locks lay in disorder, so that he looked like he had just risen from his bed rather than that he would soon seek it.

She watched him, her pulse quickening. Oh, but didn't he look wickedly tempting—and even more tasty than an almond cake.

Turning toward her, he hissed, "You're supposed to be delighted to see me."

Remembering her role—but disagreeing with his interpretation of it—she gave a nod then lifted her voice into a harsh shrill, "It's a wedding you promised me—so don't you go thinkin' I'll settle for those trinkets. It's a proper missus I'm looking to be, Mr. Theodore Winslow, and mistress here! I'll not settle for anything less, so don't you think you're going to fob me off!"

He stared at her, his expression blank with surprise, so she gestured to him, trying to encourage him to pick up on her ploy. He was supposed to be the infatuated one here. Understanding finally spread across his handsome features, and he nodded back at her, but with a glint in his eyes.

He raised his voice, his tone a touch stiff, "Of course, my sweet Sweet. Anything you wish! Just allow me to press my lips to yours."

With a click, he shut the door. Molly shook her head. "You're father's not half fooled by any of this, you know."

Theo strode across the room, then he leaned against the carved post at the foot of the bed and grinned. "Nonsense. He may be fishing the waters to see what he can catch, but his bait won't take. I've already been to see the local vicar and his spectacles just about fell off when I told him what I wanted. I also encouraged him to take his reservations to my father, so he'd stop bleating at me."

Theo frowned at that. Bad enough to have his father trying to manage his life—and Terrance's—but it was beyond bearing for Vicar Meers to try to stick his long nose into it. Particularly when the fault for everything lay at his daughter's door.

Molly shook her head again, her red curls tumbled loose and glinting in the candlelight. "At least he cares about you. And I can't imagine that many would welcome the likes of me as your wife."

Theo grinned. "Lady Thorpe seemed to like you—or so I heard from the gossip at the inn today."

The blush rose from her bare throat and spread into her cheeks. Not a hot red, but a becoming pink that gave that white skin of hers vibrancy. He decided he liked making her blush, so he unfolded his arms and came closer, sitting down on the edge of her bed.

"Word does travel fast around here," she said. Then she tucked her knees up to her chest, and sat there, mouth prim, almost as if she had never had a fellow sitting on her bed.

Or as if he planned something utterly immoral.

But they had business to discuss. Of course, her sitting there with a frill of lace peaking out from a rather fetching dressing robe which showed the tempting valley between her breasts did stir other ideas, but that would have to wait. Only the image of those lovely legs of hers kept intruding as well.

"Yes, but I didn't come here to talk to you about Lady Thorpe. I'm going to need more from you than I thought I would."

She offered a skeptical gaze from the corner of her eyes. "Your father already didn't act as you thought he would, so I don't know what more we can do."

"Leave that to me. Your part is to be quite vulgar—remember. Make it clear you'd strip me and the estate clean if you got your claws into it."

The skepticism in her eyes deepened. "If I'm that awful, how could anyone think you enamored of me? And, anyway, if you wanted all that, you ought to have hired a real actress!"

Put out by her criticism, he frowned at her. "Don't you think I tried? I had one of 'em turn me down because she'd been offered a role in some nonsense called *Czar of the Docklands* or something at Sadler's Wells—just like an actress to think that more important than a fellow's life! And the other—well, let's just say that Sallie seemed a more reasonable person to deal with. But none of that has to do with us—you're the girl I hired, and if my father sees there's a hot-blooded infatuation between us that's utterly addled me, that's why you can be grasping as the devil. . . ." he offered a grin. ". . . for I am besotted!"

"Addled more like! And just how much 'hot blood' did you have in mind showing him?"

His smile warmed. "For a start, you'll have to stop glaring at me as you are doing now. And if we're seen kissing and with my hands on your. . . ."

"Now, just a minute, I'm a good . . . good business woman," Molly said, hastily amending her words. She had been about to say she was a good girl, but that wasn't what she was supposed to be. And what with him sitting so close to her and the pleasantly masculine scent of him winding around her, she was having trouble remembering just what she was. "We made our bargain in London. And now here you are wanting extras—extra time, and extra . . . extra liberties."

"Liberties!" He glared at her, blue eyes darkening. "As if I've take a single one with you—and the bargain you made was to get me disowned. You'll not do that by acting standoffish."

"Well, I. . . ."

"Oh, come now—it's only a few kisses. That's all you need agree to."

"Nothing more?"

"Look, I'll demonstrate. That is if I may have your permission, madam?"

He didn't wait for her permission, but rose and took her hands, pulling her to her feet. She glared at him from the corner of her eyes, but as he had a firm grip on her, she had no choice but to stand up or fall into him, and she rather suspected he was hoping for the latter.

Settling his arms around her waist, he abruptly dragged her close then asked, his tone all innocence, "Now, is this so bad?"

Her pulse skittered, but she tried to stare up at him as if she'd been held so close by dozens of gentlemen. Even if she had, however, she suspected her heart might still be racing in this particular case.

Since she had nowhere to put her hands, she braced them on his chest—and found the strength of hard muscle under her touch delightful. No wonder Sallie's girls found it hard to keep hearts and heads untangled. She knew she ought to act the cold jade, but she didn't feel cold—heat surged through her, spreading from where his body pressed against hers, and from her palms, up into her arms and then across her chest.

A tingling spiraled loose inside her.

"You can do that much," she allowed, her voice almost steady and level.

Leaning down, he brushed his lips across her neck, then asked, his words half muffled by her skin, "And this?"

Her knees softened, loosened along with the rest of her. She tried to stiffen them, but her body seemed to have other ideas just now. "I don't think I. . . ."

"Oh, for . . . blazes, but I'm paying the bill here, and if it's a few kisses it takes to get my father to turn me out, then it's a few kisses you're going to have to allow, my girl."

She stared at him, wide-eyed. His eyes looked almost black as he glared at her.

Without warning, he bunched her hair in one hand and with the other he captured her chin. And then his mouth lowered to cover hers.

Ten

She tasted of apricots. Blazes, but that's just what she was like—lush and ripe and soft and round. She folded into his arms with a soft whimper—only this was no muffled cry of resistance, but a warm, welcoming sound of pleasure.

Her arms came about his neck, pulling him to her. Yet, for all the experience she must have, she kissed like a girl—awkward with where to fit her nose, her lips closed. Nibbling gently on that lush mouth, he teased his way deeper, his own desire rising as her lips parted.

Then he wanted more.

Pulling away, his breath uneven, he stared down at her. Her eyes seemed enormous—and thick, red-tinged lashes swept down over the green, veiling her gaze.

He still had hold of her chin, so he nudged it up, and wound the fingers of his other hand even deeper into her curls.

Voice thick, and with her fingers playing with the strands of his hair at the back of his neck, she said, "Well, I suppose we could do a little of that—just for show, mind."

The corner of his mouth quirked. "And might I not perhaps brush my fingers across your cheek?" He matched action to his words, then said, the words torn from him, "You've skin fine as silk."

She closed her eyes and leaned into his touch. But

then she straightened and pulled back. "Ah, now, this is all going to lead to more."

He damned well hoped it would. Fitting his hands to her trim waist again, he dragged her closer, pressing soft curves against him. "Such as to my holding your body like this?"

Lowering her hands from around his neck, she braced the heels of her palms against his chest and stared up at him, sharp reason returning to her eyes.

"You can't afford this, ducks."

"How do you know? Name your price for how much to cup my hands around your naked breasts and feel their softness?" Lifting his hands, he ran them down her sides, brushing his fingertips against the outside swell of her breasts before he tightened his hold on her waist again.

Color stained her cheeks almost as if she were embarrassed by such intimacy, but her breath quickened to match the pounding that had started in him. Yet, still she held him back.

Blazes, but she could drive a man to think of marriage—or anything else to get her into his bed.

Voice not quite steady, but with a disapproving amusement, she said, "D'you think I'll sell my favors piecemeal? Like bargains at a street fair?"

He grinned. "Oh, you're a bargain—a fair, sweet bargain. We fit well together—you can feel it, too. I know you can. Come, let me spend the night with you, my sweet Sweet."

She shook her head, and said again, "You can't afford it."

"Then name something I can afford? Perhaps to undress you? Just to see you stand naked in the firelight? Or how much to slip my hands along the length of your leg and trace the lines from ankles to the backs of your knees and up to those delicious round hips? Or to lay kisses each place where I touch? How much for all that?"

She wet her lips. He could see the pulse pounding in the hollow of her throat. "Two hundred pounds."

He grinned. "And how much more to lay with you?"

"A thousand," she shot back.

"A what!" He pushed her back. "Not even a discount for what I've already paid?"

She shook her head, and the red of her curls danced. "I told you—I'm a good business woman."

Frustration pooled in him. Almost he blurted out that he'd pay her price—any price—to lay with her now. Only he fought to cool his senses. He'd feel a damn fool in the morning to have promised so much for what he could have from any tavern wench for a few shillings. Only she wasn't a tavern wench. No, there had been times over these past few days when he had almost forgotten she was a woman for hire. She had the manners to fool almost anyone into thinking her more a lady than a Cyprian. Blazes, no wonder she commanded such prices, for she had the best skill he had ever seen—or tasted— of pretended innocence.

He would swear that kiss had stirred the same passion in her as she ignited in him. Only he could not really judge with her what was real.

And a thousand to satisfy his curiosity about that seemed beyond any sense.

But he wished he had the money to throw away on her.

With a crooked smile, he let her go. He was still half-tempted to take her up on paying two hundred to see her stripped bare, but she had pegged it right—it wouldn't stop there. So he would try to content himself with the kisses and stolen touches she had agreed to give.

Either that or mortgage his soul.

Stepping away, he said, "You set a fierce price."

For a moment, he could swear she almost looked disappointed. Which meant he had some hope that he might yet charm more from her—without the pounds spent. Well, then he would leave her tonight—and he would see what tomorrow brought.

He flicked her nose with one finger. "Good night, my sweet Sweet."

He started for the door, but as his hand touched the cool, brass knob, her voice stopped him.

"I've never been kissed like that—I mean, that is . . . well, I just want you to know it was a special moment. I mean that."

Glancing back at her, he saw that she stood with one arm wrapped about the bedpost, her head tilted and that glorious red hair spilling loose.

Lord, but she tempted. Only he had hold of himself once more. He sketched a bow. "I'll have sweet dreams tonight, my Molly."

Then he was gone, and Molly hugged the bedpost even tighter, as if it might keep her upright and not melting into a sizzling puddle.

She was the one besotted, to allow such liberties. She pressed one hand to her hot cheek to where his fingers had touched. And then to lips still tender from that kiss. Oh, and then to have told him it was a special moment.

She put a hand over her eyes.

All just to see him smile.

But, well, she had wanted him to know that he was a special person. Folks needed to be told that, and if his father had ever told him that, then Theo and his father probably wouldn't be at loggerheads now.

Only that was nothing to do with her, either.

She would just have to be more careful. Far, far more careful. He had the experience she lacked. If she allowed him too many freedoms, he would soon know her for a fraud. So she ought to keep him at arm's length and not let him guess her as a virgin who knew about as much of love-making as a nun.

Only none of her wanted to heed such sensible thoughts.

She knew what went on between a gentleman and a woman he hired—it had been impossible to avoid seeing what went on in Sallie's house, or hearing it.

Who was to say she couldn't have just a bit of fun. After all, she knew her way around a hot stove and an open fire, so there was hope here that she might play a bit with both and not get burned.

And if that's not wishful thinking, Molly-may, I don't know what is!

Theo came downstairs early, whistling, only to be met by his glowering father in the breakfast room.

He broke off his tune as soon as the squire glared at him over the top of *The London Times*. At least the dogs offered a good morning to him, tongues lolling, panting happily, and ready to lick his hand or lean against his legs.

Theo gave his father a nod, and the squire snapped his paper straight and disappeared behind it. With a shrug, Theo took up a plate and set to filling it from the sideboard with buttered eggs, Wiltshire bacon, and smoked kippers. After pouring himself a tankard of ale from the pottery jug, he settled himself at the table with the dogs tucking themselves at his feet.

"So what did you think of Miss Sweet?" Theo asked.

The squire lowered his paper, offered a scornful glance at Theo, and raised it again.

Theo went on talking between bites. "I spoke to Meers. He'll start calling the banns this Sunday—all that nonsense about asking anyone if there is any reason we should not marry."

The paper snapped again and a grunt came from behind it.

His temper starting to simmer, Theo glared at the

front and back page of *The London Times*. However, he had to keep control of himself, or he would say too much, or too much of the wrong thing.

And then it struck him.

That was exactly what his father wished to do—goad him into revealing too much. Well, that trick wouldn't work. No, indeed. He would not be the first one to blink here. Let the old man think again on that!

Stretching, he manufactured a yawn. "Blazes, but that Molly can snore." His comment pulled no reaction, so he added, "I swear I'm half starved from all that exertion last night! Lord, she'll wear me to the bone before the wedding day's half here."

Still the squire said nothing, but Theo felt certain he had at least made it clear just what sort of woman he had brought home for a bride.

That cheered him and gave him reason to wolf down his food. Finishing his ale, he rose. The dogs rose as well, coming out from under the table to see what sport waited.

"I'm off for a ride."

At that, the squire glanced over his paper. "Not waiting for your intended to come downstairs?"

"Oh, she's not one for early hours," Theo said, knowing that his father despised laziness more than any other sin. "I swear, she'd stay in bed all day if she could."

This drew a disgusted snort and the squire disappeared behind his paper.

With a ruffle to each set of floppy ears, Theo strolled from the room and headed for the stables. But his food lay heavy in his stomach and his shoulders did not relax as he stepped out of the breakfast room. Blazes, but his father could be a damned uncomfortable man. Perhaps, just to be on the safe side, it might not be bad if he found a reason to stay out of the house for the day. And it wouldn't be such a bad thing if that forced

Molly and his father to spend some time with each other—particularly if Molly set out to do her worst.

With that, he made for the front door.

And he told himself he wasn't escaping—he was just following a wise course of avoiding too much time with his father.

Washed, with her curls caught up in a green ribbon and her striped gown freshly pressed, Molly found her way through the maze of the house. Its paths, she decided, were as confused as her feelings this morning. Part of her argued for a hard-headed stance of allowing no more intimacies such as last night's. Only that was not what she had agreed upon, nor was it really very helpful to Theo in getting himself disinheritted. Most of all, while it might be sensible, it did not fit with what she wanted.

So perhaps she could just think of her fifty pounds whenever he kissed her.

She doubted she would do that.

She did not feel a level-headed business woman when Theo had his arms around her. She felt floaty and warm and all soft in a way that had nothing to do with any sort of business. It seemed she'd been wise to avoid Sallie's trade—but would she feel this way with another gentleman?

Something about Theo stirred her. She had lain awake last night thinking about him, and her reaction to his kiss. Was it just that he was so handsome? She could stare at him all day, really. Or was it that no one had ever smiled at her with such charm? Or was she vulnerable because she had never had a beau before?

Not for lack of chance, of course. When she had left St. Marylebone's for her first position—as a scullery maid at Mr. Dillington's home at Number Seven, Great Queen Street—there had been a second footman who seemed quite taken with her. And there was the butcher in Knightsbridge now who added an extra quarter pound to her orders, and who kept the freshest sausage for her. Even Sallie had said that with her hair and figure she'd not lack for gentlemen if she wished them.

Only she had never been particularly interested.

Or had just been too particular. The second footman, even though he had had lovely blond curls, had also had the most off-putting braying laugh. And the butcher, a heavy-set man, carried with him the unattractive odor of blood and onions, which he seemed to eat raw.

But now she had gone and found herself a gentleman who was as far above her touch as were the clouds in the sky. And she was only his for hire. And for pretend.

Still, she knew herself lucky.

She might not have him for long—nor for genuine— but she had him for now. And those first few tear-filled weeks in St. Marylebone's Workhouse had taught her the wisdom of living for the moment, and not for some lost past or uncertain future.

So she would stop fretting and she'd enjoy what she could.

When it ended, she would have fifty pounds in her pocket and some lovely memories. Yes, she would.

She just hoped that proved enough.

With that settled in her mind she made for the break-fast room, the faint aromas of hot food stirring her appetite.

She paused, however, as she opened the door and saw the squire at the table—and those dogs of his. They looked larger and hungrier, today.

Lowering his paper, the squire glanced at her, then went straight back behind it. The dogs seemed to take their cue from their master for they also disappeared, darting under the table as if it were a cave for them.

Just remember he is not supposed to like you, she told herself, squaring her shoulders. *And he's certainly disagreeable enough that there's no need to have a care for him.* But it was rather a bit much that even the dogs turned their backs to her.

Shutting the door behind her, she slipped into her Sallie accent. "Coo—I'm fair famished I am."

The squire glowered at her again over the top of his paper, his eyes narrowed. And Molly almost smiled to see a copy of the expression that Theo got when he was crossed. Lord, these Winslow men! Like half-wild boys.

"Thought you slept all day," the squire said, his voice a low grumble.

She started to deny this, then it occurred to her that some of Sallie's girls indeed worked the night through and took their rest while the sun shone. Not her hours, of course.

Still, she saw no need to stray from the truth, so she said, "I'd rise from the dead, I would, for one of Mrs. Brown's meals—she's a way with food that could make a angel wish for mortal form."

With a snort, he put up his paper before him.

He had not, Molly noted, either risen in her presence as should a gentleman for a lady, nor offered to pour her coffee. Well, that certainly told what he thought of her. And showed poor manners on his part, she decided, for a real gentleman would have treated her just the same as any lady.

Clattering plates and humming, she made her selections from the sideboard—being generous with her helpings, for didn't those thin wafers of ham just look to melt on the tongue? Then she sat down.

The rattle of plates had the dogs out from under the table, and now they sat lined up on either side of her. One of them—the brown and white one—had a hopeful look in his eye as he licked his lips.

She glanced at them, then at the squire's paper. Then she tore off three bits of ham which disappeared as soft tongues lapped her fingers. She smiled at them. Well, at least she had some friends now.

"I expect Theo'll be wantin' to send somethin' to the papers about us getting married. Quite excitin' to think of my name being printed up for all t'see."

The paper lowered. Molly met the squire's harsh stare with a calm smile in place. How much would it take to make him lose his temper and throw her and Theo out? He seemed even more stubborn than his son.

She began to cut apart her smoked herring. "D'you think Theo's brother'll come to the wedding? I'd quite like that."

With a snap the paper rose again. "I've only one son."

Molly's fork clattered onto the china. The noise startled the dogs into ducking under the table and drew the squire from behind his paper barricade.

"Just like that—" Molly said, staring at him. "You're willing to throw a child away? Well, of all the—why I wouldn't waste a single relation if I had one! And that's not just from being an orphan."

With a snort, he thrust up his paper again.

Molly's eyes narrowed. Thickening her Sallie accent, she hoped for the worst. If he threw her out now she would happily dance out the door with Theo. And she would know she had done Theo the greatest good in helping him out from under the influence of such a disagreeable old man. "I plan to be a proper sister, I do, to Theo's brother. So Terrance'll be welcome here when I'm mistress."

With an abrupt movement, the squire flattened his paper onto the table next to his coffee cup and glared at her. "You're . . . you're impertinent!"

She forced a broad smile and patted her curls. "Why, ducks, ain't that just dear of you. I ain't ever been called that afore."

The squire's face flushed a splotchy red, and Molly

watched, a little worried now. "Here now—you aren't going to have an apoplexy on me, are you?"

Scraping his chair back against the wooden floor, the squire pushed himself from the table and stood scowling at her, black bushy eyebrows tight. She lifted her chin, unwilling to allow him to bully her.

Imagine him casting off his own son—and for what?

What, indeed, she wondered? Oh, gracious, she hoped Theo's brother had not done something so dastardly as to deserve this treatment.

Then she thought of how Theo had spoken of his brother—there had been nothing but admiration in his tone, and she could not imagine he would think so well of a brother who had committed some horrible crime.

So she glared back at the squire.

For a moment, his mouth worked, almost as if he was chewing the words he wanted to spit at her. Then he turned and strode out, his boots clomping and his dogs clattering after him, their nails skittering on the wood. The heavy oak door shut behind him with an ominous, soft click.

Letting out a breath, Molly slumped in her chair, her appetite gone and her insides shaking. Well, Theo wouldn't be able to say she had not done her best today to make herself unwanted.

However, she did not have the chance that day to tell Theo of her exchange with his father. They met only just before dinner, and before she could say anything, the squire came in, black eyebrows as low as storm clouds, his mouth set in a line, his blue eyes snapping with irritation.

Theo kissed her hand and did his best to act the lover—and very distracting it was, too. Only not so distracting that she could ignore the squire's sullen mood, which settled around them like a heavy, chilling mist. Even the dogs seemed to sense it, for they kept themselves tucked into the corners of the room.

She found it a relief to escape, her dinner hardly touched, and she thought if that continued, she would be taking in Jane's dresses as well as having had to take them up.

The next two days did continue with Theo making himself scarce, and Molly could only wish she might, too. She tried to make a game of it with the squire. She would roll the dice and move her piece, and then the squire would take his turn, pitting his will against hers. And they would play until one of them ran all their pieces off the board—only she was not certain which of them that would be.

He was not only a stubborn man, he was as bitter as cold tea. It amazed her that he could have the utter adoration of even so much as one of his dogs.

In the evenings, she at least had Theo's company. And he stole kisses from her when he encountered her on the stairs or alone in a room. That, however, did not help. It left her feeling like dough wound up in a twist.

On the third day of this, she actually considered fleeing the house herself, for she longed for even a momentary rest from this perpetual anxiety. She had the excuse, after all, of having promised Lady Thorpe to visit. Only at the thought of slipping out, guilt stung her. She was here to earn her money.

However, she was also finding it impossible to eat in company, and she was half-starved. So she fled to the only haven she had ever known in her life—the kitchen.

Arming herself with Lady Thorpe's recipe for almond cake—for at least that gave her an excuse to venture into Mrs. Brown's domain—Molly found her way to the back of the house. She hoped she would find Mrs. Brown alone. If Simpson was there, or any of the other oh-so-superior staff, she would not stay. She just could not take any more disapproving or curious stares, not and try to take so much as a bite of anything.

However, stepping into the kitchen, she found it a

bright, high-ceilinged room, blessedly empty of anything
other than pots, a cheerful fire and something that
smelled of meat cooking bubbling in an iron pot that
hung over the hearth fire to her left.

The stone walls had been plastered and painted white.
Copper pots hung neatly from hooks on the ceiling, car-
rots lay stacked on a well-scrubbed table in the middle of
the room and it all looked tidy and inviting.

With her nose twitching, Molly stepped into the room
and took up an iron hook from the fender to swing the
pot out from the fire. Putting her face into the steam, she
breathed in the aroma from the bubbling mixture. Soup,
she gathered, already starting to wonder what spices had
been added, and wishing she had a spoon to taste it.

She had just begun to glance around the room for a
ladle or some such thing, when a firm step on the stone
floor made her straighten, her cheeks warm for being
where she had no right to be.

A tall, slender woman dressed in brown stopped in the
doorway and stared at her, gray eyes wide in an angular
face. Her high-waisted white apron, neatly starched, and
her lace-trimmed cap at once told her status as cook, and
Molly found herself blinking in surprise. This woman
looked only a year or more older than herself, banishing
the image she had been building of Mrs. Brown as
ample, aged, and kind.

The woman's mouth puckered at once. Then, hands
folded prim before her, she said, her tone pricking like
the edge of a knife, "You should have rung if you wished
something from the kitchen."

Molly struggled for an excuse, but could only find the
truth. "If I had, that'd only bring Simpson scowling at
me, and I am sorry for poking my nose into your soup,
but it smelled too good to resist. Lamb?"

A reluctant answer came. "Beef bones for carrot soup."

"Oh, but there's lamb in it, I'd swear it."

Mrs. Brown's eyebrows rose. "Well, I use a bit of mutton—only for flavor."

"And turnips, onions . . ." Molly's eyes narrowed as she considered the aromas. "And something else, I'd swear."

"Marjoram," Mrs. Brown said, her tone cautious and her glance now suspicious.

"Ah—I'd not thought of that. A very nice touch. But I'm intruding, and I only meant to bring you this." She stuck out a hand with the recipe. "It's for Lady Thorpe's almond cakes."

With her mouth still puckered, Mrs. Brown reached out and tentatively took the recipe. She unfolded the paper, glanced at Molly, and then began to scan the sheet, her eyes sharpening with interest. "Orange-flower water! I knew it."

Molly smiled. "Ah, I thought you might appreciate it."

Mrs. Brown glanced up, her expression severe again. "Why is that?"

"You'd never serve such a duck as you did the other night if you couldn't. Duck's so easy to come out greasy or tough. And it needs just the right sauce; and the currant was lovely."

Mrs. Brown's mouth softened. "You seem to know your way around a kitchen."

"Well, why not be interested in food—we all have to eat. And I wish I could, only between the squire and Simpson, it's hard to manage a swallow of anything. Which is why I've been sending your dishes back—please don't think it reflects on your talent."

The faintest of militant glimmer shone in Mrs. Brown's gray eyes. "Simpson glowered at me for four months after I took on the job from Mrs. Rummer."

"Was she the cook before?"

"Aye. Plain and simple was her motto—took me three months after she retired to even slip in so much as a curry."

"Oh, you do curries—I've not had a proper one since I was a girl in India. Other than what I cook myself. But I'd rather eat someone else's—if I cook it, I taste too much to want to sit down after for a meal."

"India was it?" Hesitant interest stirred in Mrs. Brown's eyes and Molly's heart lifted. The woman still looked uncomfortable, but perhaps they might just manage a truce.

And then Mrs. Brown asked, with only a little doubt in her tone, "I don't suppose you've a recipe for a mulagatawny soup?"

Eleven

Molly brightened at once, and she began to talk about the foods of India and the dishes she had learned to cook as a girl for her uncle—Madras lamb, sag or spinach, dal or lentils. Her uncle had disliked the spiced native foods, but Molly soon learned that the combinations of spices could be used to soothe as well as to stimulate. The household cook—an elderly woman with silver hair and dark skin and a red dot on her forehead—had been willing to teach Molly, and she learned ways to use spices to tempt any appetite.

Since then, Molly had felt an obligation to be as ready to pass on such knowledge, only she had found few interested.

So she began to talk now of what she knew.

It wasn't long until Mrs. Brown offered up a taste of her broth—serving up a bowl of it, actually, and asking for suggestions. Then nothing would do for her but to take down the tea canister, unlock it, and set a pot brewing.

With them comfortable around the kitchen table in high-backed wooden chairs—and with Molly stuffed on Mrs. Brown's biscuits, and Mrs. Brown's leather-bound household book now six pages thicker with Molly's knowledge of cumin, turmeric, and coriander for curry, saffron for rice, and which peppers to use with which meats—it seemed to Molly as if they had known each other for years.

"The Hindu," she said, taking another biscuit, "believe

food can balance temperament to keep a body in harmony. Hot foods stimulate hot tempers."

"Then I'd best throw out my peppers for this household," Mrs. Brown said, her tone dry.

Molly grinned. "Pitta is what the Hindu would say—all fire and no air or water. I'd wager Theo's brother's the same, for all the trouble he seems to have caused. And here's Theo—"

She broke off. She had almost confided about Theo's plan to get himself disinherited.

Mrs. Brown seemed not to notice. She only poured fresh tea from the pot, then settled back in her chair. "Well, I don't like to gossip, but I will say the squire brought this on his own head. I grew up hearabouts—started off a between-maid under Mrs. Rummer—and after Mrs. Winslow died, the squire let those lads of his run wild."

"So you knew Theo's mother?"

"I did that—lovely lady. Elegant as a willow, and just as frail. Her husband's temper used to lay her flat with the megrims so that she was forever going off to some watering place for a cure. Only one time she didn't come back. Or least the squire came home with only her mortal remains to bury. Buried his heart too, that's what Mrs. Rummer used to swear."

"How awful," Molly said, thinking of the death of her parents and her uncle, and how little sympathy she had felt for the squire. It would be harder to judge him harshly now.

"What was awful was how he locked himself in his shooting room and wouldn't see no one for weeks after. Word went around that he might shoot himself, but he finally came out and he took to drink something fierce. Mrs. Rummer swore he'd end buried in a bottle or breakin' his neck on one of those horses of his, but he hasn't so far. However, I say—and so did Mrs. Rummer—

that if he'd taken a proper interest in his sons, his eldest wouldn't have ended in such trouble and the youngest wouldn't be looking to follow his brother's path."

Molly frowned. "Terrance didn't go so far as to murder anyone did he?"

"No—but it might have been less fuss if he had." Pausing, Mrs. Brown glanced toward the doorway, then leaned forward. "He ran off with Mr. Meers's daughter—he's the vicar, as you may know. 'Course, not that she's what I'd call a pious miss—not a bit of it. But Mr. Terrance ought not to have left her in Brighton! Particularly not when he's her third cousin."

"Gracious—well, I see why that might upset his father. But to disinherit him!"

"It might not have come to that, only Mr. Meers tracked his girl down and found her being kept in some inn by a military fellow—well on her way to being nothing more than a. . . ." she broke off, her mouth puckering.

"A woman such as myself?" Molly suggested. "You need not think I have any feelings to hurt there. It's not a trade I'd wish for any woman, so I do feel for this poor girl. Did her father take her back?"

"He did—true Christian charity. You have to admit that. But that's when the real trouble started. He was for telling everyone he'd go to the law and sue for damages, he would, and I heard the squire had to pay a dear sum to put a stop to it. Then Mr. Terrance wouldn't so much as answer a single note from the squire to return home and account for himself, decent-like. That's what really did for Mr. Terrance, if you ask me. For the squire to be touched in his pocket and not have so much as the satisfaction of ringing a proper fury down on his son's head—well. . . ."

She shook her head and stirred her tea. "The squire was in a proper fit when he sent for Mr. Braysworth—he's the solicitor, but you wouldn't know that. Not a bit of the land's entailed, so the squire could cut out his eldest from everything—and he did, too. You could hear him shouting orders to Mr. Braysworth clear through the house, you could. But I expect Mr. Theo told you all that already."

"Well, actually—he hasn't. He gets into a proper fit himself at the mention of it. And I have to say, it still seems extreme to throw away a son like that, so I can't blame Theo really for being so angry. Oh, it's such a tangle!"

Speculation lit Mrs. Brown's eyes. "You actually care for Mr. Theo, don't you?"

Molly couldn't stop the warmth that tingled on her cheeks. She fixed her stare on her half-empty teacup, and then glanced up. The sharpness had faded from Mrs. Brown's gray eyes, replaced by curiosity. Still, the woman could gossip with the best of them, and while it would be a treat to share her troubles, Molly hesitated at confiding too much when she wondered if it would rapidly spread through the house.

So she only smiled and said, "Is there a woman in the neighborhood who can resist him?"

"Oh, there's one as I could name."

"Miss Harwood?" Molly asked, thinking of Sylvain Harwood's comment that Theo had been interested in her sister.

"So you've heard—did Mr. Theo tell you of her?"

Molly shook her head.

"I'm not surprised. I doubt he even thinks of her anymore, really. Cecila Harwood was the prettiest girl in the neighborhood, but flighty as a pheasant in shooting season. Nothing but a relief—even for Mr. Theo, if you ask me—to see her married off. And I wish her well of it, and hope she found a gent who can settle her."

"But now Theo's brought me home—is that out of the pan and into the fire?"

Mrs. Brown tipped her head and regarded Molly, her stare so direct it almost unsettled. "A day ago, I'd have said yes, but now—well, let's just say that maybe this pot ought to simmer a bit more before I can tell if it's to my taste or not."

Things were not going well, Theo decided, as he dressed for dinner.

He had been out on George—his favorite hunter—for most of the day, but had not found his usual relief in such escape. All day he had worried over Molly. How was she faring? Was his father being abrupt with her, or avoiding her? What, in fact, was she doing during the day? He had stayed out until his seat was even sorer from the saddle than yesterday, his stomach grumbling, and his head beginning to ache.

Of course, his head had ached for the past two days— and not from either hunger or the aftereffect of strong spirits, though his father was enough to encourage any fellow to find relief in a bottle. Only there'd been no appeal in any thought of venturing to The Four Feathers for a pint, for someone would ask about his wedding, and he didn't want to talk about that. Nor did he want to hear lewd speculation about Molly.

Damnation, this entire scheme ought to be over and done so he could get back to a bit of fun!

Still, he'd been shooting with his father enough times to know him for a canny, patient sportsman who usually managed to outdo his sons in what game he bagged. But Theo was not going to let the squire best him in this.

Scowling at his reflection and the mangled cravat that now hung in a limp mess about his neck, Theo wondered if he ought to have hired himself a valet when he had last been in London. He had thought about it, only it had seemed such a nuisance to have around, and an expense. Terrance didn't have a valet, after all—only Burke to look after his horses for him.

Unknotting the cravat, Theo tugged on the bellpull to

summon help. At least he could do something about this without having to wait.

A few minutes later, one of the footmen—Albert— knocked and entered. After glancing over the servant's dapper turn-out to his livery, Theo thrust a fresh length of starched linen at him. "See what you can do with this."

The footman looked surprised, but stepped forward to create a neat enough tie that Theo gave him an approving smile and tipped him a shilling.

His mood improved, he went downstairs.

Then he found himself the first to enter the drawing room.

He glanced around the room, scowling. Blast it, but he wanted Molly there. He wanted some time with her before his father came. In fact, now that he thought of it, those few days with her before his father had come home had been . . . well, they had been nice.

But none of that has anything to do with the plan, he reminded himself. And he could almost wish that plan—and Terrance with it—at perdition. Only he couldn't really. It wasn't what one did with a brother.

Straightening, he thought about going up to Molly's room. He might, with some luck, catch her half-dressed. He smiled at that, but reason intruded. Even if he did find her in her shift, she'd probably have a maid to help her, and what he really wanted was to be the only one helping her undress.

Restless now, he stalked over to the decanters and poured himself a glass of burgundy. Then he stood beside the open window, for the evening had warmed turning almost muggy. That didn't help. He kept thinking of Molly. Wondering if her hair was still down. It had been glorious to see it loose and glinting in the candlelight, and to wind his fingers into its softness.

He drank some of his wine.

Really, he had been wrong to leave this matter entirely

to her. She was just a bit of a thing really—plucky, yes, but he ought not to have thrown her into his father's path and stood back. Uneasy with such thoughts, he started to pull at the cravat that Albert had tied, then stopped himself.

No sense having spent the time letting the fellow tie it only to tear it apart. And there was no sense, either, in having set his plan to force his father into accepting Terrance as his heir again only to tear it apart by not following through.

Drinking his wine, he made up his mind. It might not be pleasant, but he'd just have to take a stronger role in matters. And, blazes, but he wanted to see more of Molly. He couldn't do that if he stayed out on a horse all day.

Frowning at the gathering twilight outside the house, he wondered just why, anyway, he had allowed his father to drive him away. And he saw suddenly that was what had always happened with Terrance. He had simply copied that pattern.

There had been a time, of course, when he could recall wanting to please the squire, to earn his praise. But he was quick to learn that nothing he did ever earned an ounce of notice, and so he had looked to Terrance. Now he saw how he had sought his brother's approval, earning it by copying how Terrance did everything—even losing his temper and storming off.

Why carry on with that now?

Of course, his father could make a room—or a house— damned uncomfortable with his moods. Certainly a good reason to avoid him. But, likewise, Molly could make a fellow feel a number of other things, all of them quite pleasant. He started to smile. Blazes, if he kept his focus on her, who gave a damn what his father was doing.

His thoughts were still on those attractive aspects of Molly when his father came into the drawing room, trailed by Caesar, Marcus, and Plato. Theo tousled silky ears as each dog thrust his head into an outstretched hand for a greeting, and then he gave his father a cheerful enough hello.

And when Molly stepped in, Theo came forward, the pleasure genuine behind his smile.

"You look a rare treat," he said, setting down his wine glass so he could take her hands. And she did, done up in that red gown that hugged her curves in ways no proper gown should, giving her a glossy sheen like a ripe apple.

He kissed each hand, watching how the blush spilled up from her throat and across the translucent skin of her cheeks. That had to be her most amazing skill. He really would have to ask her sometime how she managed such a show of innocence.

For now, he contented himself with steering her to a seat near the window and the cooling breeze and asking about her day, and teasing her now for her resistance to learning how to ride.

"I could take you out tomorrow on a slow, very short donkey. That'll at least get you astride something."

She made a face. "If you want to take me someplace, then I'd rather you offer that picnic you promised."

"Shall I? You only have to tell me your favorite foods and I'll have Mrs. Brown prepare them all for you."

"But I've no favorites—or at least, I don't have any unfavorites when it comes to her cooking."

"Then we're going to have a lot to eat for she'll have to cook everything she knows, and you can sample a bite of each and set your favorites."

She smiled at him, and he thought that put a gleam in her eyes like sunlight glinting on a meadow. Before he could turn the thought into words, the squire cleared his throat and demanded to know if Theo had settled the other details of his wedding.

Not caring to be distracted from Molly, Theo an-

swered absently that there was still time for all that, then
turned back to his sweet Sweet.

The squire watched this exchange, uneasy for the first
time since he had come home and had heard the tale
from Simpson of the unsuitable woman that Theo had
brought home.

As soon as he had seen his son and the girl together,
he had known it to be some mad lark. The lad was too
young, yet, to think of tying himself to any female—why,
only look at how his seeming interest in the Harwood
girl had been nothing more than boyish infatuation.
This would prove the same—and he could swear he had
already seen Theo's interest wane over the past few days.

*Just don't give him something to push against, and he'll soon
fall out of it.*

Now he wondered about that, for something else lay
in the air between these two tonight. He noted how
Theo bent close to say something to this tart of his, his
tone low, for her ears only. And how she looked at him,
a dancing light in her eyes that'd be enough to start a
fire in any man. Why had he not noticed this before?

But it wouldn't last. The boy was taken in by a curvaceous figure and a clever woman's skills—you could see at
a glance that this one had more thoughts than did any
man good. She was a schemer, right enough. He had been
tempted a half dozen times to toss her out—only he knew
Theo would follow her, and he had no sons left to spare.

Still, the girl had spirit. She wasn't one of those wilting
types—and that twisted the old pain inside him as nothing else had in years.

Turning aside, he poured himself a glass of wine, drank
it, and poured another. Then, unable to stop himself, he
glanced at his son and the lad's intended—rubbish that
anything would come of it. He need only wait and let
Theo tire of her vulgar ways.

He kept telling himself that throughout dinner.

With Theo's full attention fixed on her, the girl blossomed as she had not on the other evenings. She flirted and joked, and the squire had to fight the impulse to smile himself at some of her more outrageous jests. They showed a coarse sort of humor that didn't suit a young lady, but she wasn't a lady, even though she seemed too young for her trade. *Ought to be in some schoolroom,* the squire thought, glaring at her. Only there was that figure of hers which showed a woman's maturity and allure.

She didn't turn to see his disapproval, and she was, in fact, off with some new story—this one about India and monkeys—that the squire fought not to listen to.

No wonder the lad's fascinated, he thought, covertly eyeing those glowing red curls, the expanses of white skin displayed by a scandalous gown, and the curve of her lips. He forced a frown. Infatuations never lasted. This would be no different. He, better than anyone, knew the cruel truth of that.

He noted, too, that she slipped bits of meat to the dogs when she thought no one was paying attention. And he realized then that all of 'em—Caesar, Marcus, and Plato—had started to attach themselves to her during mealtimes.

A soft touch, he thought. *Soft and bright as new copper.* She'd brought smiles and laughter back into this house.

He deepened his scowl.

Far better she had never come with a reminder of feminine graces—and brought back to him what his cursed disposition had made him lose forever.

The patter of rain on the windows woke Molly. She lay with her eyes closed, dreams fading—they had been such nice ones with Theo kissing her. Then she smiled. He had kissed her—just once on the stairs last night, before his father had come across them and had dragged

Theo off, saying something about wanting to talk about the harvest schedules for the home farm.

Theo had left her with reluctance, but for the first time she had also noticed that he had not turned sullen and brooding under the lash of his father's abrupt tone. In fact, he had not even seemed to care about his father's mood.

Something had shifted in him. In a rather interesting fashion. He had seemed . . . well, older almost. She had wondered if he might stop by her room later, and she had thought she might ask him about it, but he had not.

And that is just as well for me.

Dreams of kisses seemed far safer just now that the actual ones—though they weren't half as nice.

With a yawn, she opened her eyes and stretched. Today they were to picnic.

Then she sat upright and stared at the window.

Rain continued pattering down on the pane, streaking the glass. Slipping from the warmth of her bed, she ran to the window, a wet chill in the room slipping around her bare legs. It had to be just a slight summer wetting, which blew out just as quickly as it blew in.

Gray skies, muddy lanes, and dripping trees told a different story. It looked ready to rain in earnest for the rest of the day. Somerset, she decided, had worse weather than London.

To cheer herself, she put on her favorite gown. One of her own for a change—in purple chiffon silk over a purple silk underskirt, with ruffles about the square neckline and sleeves. She had found it at a stall in Covent Garden which sold used dresses—some discarded from wealthy houses, some given to maids and then sold to supplement salaries, and some very likely pilfered from the closets of ladies who had more dresses than they could count. This one had cost her dear—four pounds and ten from her savings. An extravagance, but one she had never regretted, for she adored the dress and that it fit almost as if made for her.

Feeling cheered, she found the breakfast room empty and settled down to enjoy her morning.

By the time she finished her last sip of tea, she had begun to wonder if the squire had kept Theo with him all night and the morning through. Neither of them had appeared downstairs. With nothing else to do, and poor weather for doing anything outside, she wandered the house, looking at portraits.

Every other painting seemed to be of a horse or a dog. She soon grew tired of reading the brass plates that gave their names and sometimes their pedigrees. The people in the paintings seemed not to deserve any such notice—or perhaps it was assumed that anyone looking at them would know who they were. Most had the look of Winslows—straight, autocratic noses, tall foreheads, stubborn chins, and a good number of them with those startling blue eyes.

None as handsome as Theo, however.

When she tired of walking, she made her way to a room that had a number of books. Not so many as to be called a library, but more than in the rest of the rooms that she had seen. Her education had not been overlooked at St. Marylebone's—numbers and reading were taught to everyone, as was a careful hand. However, the only reading encouraged had been the Bible, for books were dear to buy, as was a subscription to a lending library.

However, Sallie considered it part of her calling for all her girls to be able to carry on a conversation about anything that might interest a gentleman, including politics, literature, and history even. To that end, on Sunday afternoons Sallie read from every fashionable work she could find, and encouraged lively discussions afterwards.

Molly had often taken away the books to read on her own.

Now, as she searched for something to interest, all she found were books and magazines on hunting, shooting, boxing, fishing, and the occasional thick volume with a long title that seemed to deal with farming.

Theo found her still prowling the room, searching the shelves.

"What in blazes are you doing?" he asked.

She had climbed up onto a chair in order to see the titles of the works on the higher shelves. Glancing down at him, she said, "Don't you have anything to read that doesn't involve either killing some animal, or digging up the ground?"

One black eyebrow lifted and he said, scorn thick in his tone, "Read? I thought we were having a picnic?"

She started to climb down from the chair, but he came to her and put his hands on her waist, holding her in place. With her feet sinking into the soft cushions of the chair, she stood just a little taller than he.

"I think I like having you look up to me," she said, unable to resist teasing him, and her pulse quickening at his touch.

"So it's a pedestal you want after all? Shall I get you a proper one—all white marble and high enough that I can kiss your toes?"

She wrinkled her nose. "I don't aim for great heights."

"But you might like your toes being kissed and nibbled on."

Pulling back, she tilted her head to the side. "It sounds a bit ticklish."

"And is this ticklish?" he asked, then pulled her close to kiss the hollow of her throat.

Closing her eyes, she leaned into the sensation. Then she straightened with a reminder to think about her fifty pounds. "Here now—I thought you said something about a picnic?"

He pulled away with a grin, his eyes sparkling with mischief. "I'm going to have to start calling you my hungry Molly—how can you eat like a trencher and not weigh in at twenty stone?"

"I don't eat like a trencher. But I could just now."

With a laugh, he took hold of her waist and swung her off the chair, then once around before setting her on the ground. She clutched his neck, half out of breath from the surprise of it.

"You *are* a dangerous fellow!"

He flicked her chin with a finger. "Not a bit—tame as a lamb. Now, I've promised you a picnic, and it's a picnic you shall have."

She glanced at the windows as he started to lead her from the room. "We'll be soaked through."

With a grin, he kept hold of her hand and started up the stairs. "So little faith. Close your eyes. Come along— closed, I said. You'll have to hold tight and trust me."

"I already do too much," she muttered, but then she shut her eyes tight.

Where he led her, she could not tell. She lost track after the stairs turned twice, and then it seemed to be ages down a corridor that smelled musty from lack of use. She heard a door creak open and then closed behind her. Her nose twitched with the wafting scents of food—curry, she thought. And a pork pie, and roast . . . roast what? Ah, pheasant.

She could have stood there all day with her eyes shut, breathing those tantalizing aromas.

Standing behind her, he took hold of her shoulders, then leaned close and whispered, "Now you may look."

Twleve

Theo had spent the morning arranging this, and now he waited for Molly's reaction, more eager than he would ever have thought possible. His father had kept him up late last night with excuses of estate business—and he had actually found himself growing interested in the details of managing the four hundred and sixty acres that comprised Winslow Park. Twice he'd had to stop himself from making suggestions on perhaps crossing some Romneys with their Dorset Horn sheep to improve the wool yield, or to see about replanting the aging apple orchards that lay to the south, with an eye to then selling the extra cider production.

All that was Terrance's proper business—not his. These would be Terrance's lands someday. And he was not going to be lured into thinking them his properties. No, but someday he would. . . .

His thoughts had snagged there. Just what would he do someday?

He had gone to bed grumpy—and without any reason for his snarling mood—his head too full of the brandy his father had kept pouring for them both. Restless, unable to sleep, he had then prowled to his mother's deserted rooms—and he had stood there with a candle, looking about him without even knowing what he was looking for. His past? Or his future?

Blazes, it was all nonsense—but he had felt better after

staring at the miniature of her that he had found tucked into her wardrobe, along with a few other personal items, including the pearls she had once worn. He'd been able to seek his own bed then.

And he had woken to the depressing sight of rain.

That galvanized him.

It was one bloody thing to have his schemes run into thick cover due to his father's bullheaded unwillingness to admit he'd been bested, but he was not about to see his plans for Molly ruined today by bloody rain.

So he had had the picnic spread in the old nursery.

He leaned close to her now—the scent of something flowery carried to him from her skin. "This used to be Sherwood Forest, and the Island of Madagascar—don't know why, but Terrance liked the name of the place— and just about anywhere else on a rainy day. So I thought it would do well enough for our picnic."

She glanced at him, eyes glowing, and he suddenly wanted to wrap his arms around her and bury his face in that mass of red hair as he would if she were a rose. "Oh, Theo, it's perfect."

With a shrug, he folded his hands behind him. He'd never felt awkward with a female before, but somehow the pleasure in her face, while it pleased him, also left him uncertain what to do.

"I thought the potted palms a nice touch," he said, then gestured to the plants he'd had brought up from the old conservatory. No one ever used it anymore—not since his mother had died. But the staff still maintained the plants, as they did everything else in the house.

She glanced at them, then turned and smiled up at him. "You're wonderful." Standing on tiptoe, she brushed a kiss on his cheek.

His face warmed as if it were his first kiss, and then a different hunger blazed loose in him.

But she had hold of his hand now and was tugging

him forward. "We shall sit on pillows—that's how the rajahs eat in India, you know. Sprawling in luxury on silken cushions."

"Blazes, that reminds me." He tugged out from her hold and then slipped his hand into his waistcoat pocket. "I want you to wear these."

Molly gasped as he pulled out a strand of pearls and a pair of earrings. Her eyes widened and she drew back.

"What—don't you like them?" he asked. "They were my mother's. Her favorites I think."

She shook her head, red curls bobbing. "Oh, I couldn't."

"'Course you can."

"But your father. . . ."

He let out an exasperated sigh. "That's the whole point. He's playing cagey—wants to see if I'm in earnest or not. This should show him I mean business."

Stepping closer, his jaw set, he fastened the necklace around Molly's neck. She knew better than to argue with him when he had that look on his face—she would only be wasting breath. Then he stepped back to admire the effect, and she touched a hand to the strands, self-conscious about it in a way she had not been about the ring and bracelet he had given her.

These, after all, had been his mother's. What would the squire think to see them on her?

Theo frowned at her. "They're a bit dull, aren't they?"

Automatically, she answered. "Pearls have to be worn—they take their sheen from the oils of your skin. That's what Sallie says."

A smile edged up Theo's mouth. "When it comes to jewels, I'd wager Sallie knows what she's talking about. Now, I thought you said you were hungry?"

He gave her the pearl earrings to put on and, with only a moment's hesitation, she took them. No mirror hung in this room—it wasn't a thing she could imagine that two boys had ever needed—but she managed without it.

Seated on the floor with him—with her skin warming the pearls—she decided she had indeed stepped into a moment of fantasy. And she'd enjoy it to the maximum.

Molly looked a right treat, Theo decided, as the pearls started to gleam, and with that flush of pleasure still on her cheeks. He began to serve her from the dishes laid out, and spent more time listening to her exclaim over the food than he did eating.

She had slipped into her proper accent, almost as if that was more natural to her than were her low-bred tones. A bit of pretend, perhaps, to go with this room of childhood dreams. And that startled him thinking of her stories.

"Did you actually grow up in India?" he asked, for she had been talking of the food there as if she knew it well.

She nodded, her mouth full at the moment with pastry. Smiling, he flicked the crumbs from her lower lip.

"How in blazes did you ever get to Sallie's house from there?"

Molly stared at him a moment, then took a swallow of wine to clear her throat. She took a second swallow to keep the entire truth from spilling out. Telling him of her path to being a cook in a house of harlots, with a stop in a workhouse, would only spoil the moment, so she swallowed her wine and put on a smile. "Oh, it's a long story."

He stretched out on the floor, one elbow resting on a pillow, his legs impossibly long. "We've all day."

Blinking, she stared at him. Then she took a breath and started sketching her past—just fragments really. How her father had been posted to India with the army, and had taken her and her mother with him. Her parent's death from cholera, her Uncle Fred taking her in.

"That's where I got my interest in cooking, you see, for he had finicky tastes—he liked that saying about an army traveling on its stomach, which is why he said it was no use traveling anywhere in India, for there was nothing but rice fit to eat."

"And just how old were you when he 'took you in'?" Theo asked, an odd light in his eyes.

She glanced at him—he sounded almost, well, hostile about her uncle. "Eight or nine. For I was almost twelve when the fever took him. It was going through Fort George in Madras like a hot wind. And when he realized he wasn't going to recover, he booked passage to England for me, then wrote my mother's people to meet me—only they never did."

He frowned, and she almost smiled at his expression. It did sound dramatic, she supposed, but it all seemed so very long ago, and almost as if it had happened in a different lifetime.

"Didn't you have their direction from your uncle?" he asked.

Thinking of how badly prepared she had been—with that scrawl of a note from Uncle Fred, for the fever had had him then, no money really, for it had been spent on her passage, and with only the very few things her parents had left her—she gave a shrug. She had indeed set off for England with nothing more than a hope. However, she had also long ago given up the game of "if only."

"I did," she said. "They wrote letters at the workhouse to the address I gave, but the answer came back that no one knew any Captain or Amelia Sweet. Or perhaps no one wanted to know. There'd been a rift of some sort, and either it ran too deep, or they'd moved on without a thought to her."

With a shake of his head, he put his wine glass down. "No wonder you thought me mad to be courting a split within my own family."

She glanced down to swirl her wine, then looked up again and tried to make a joke of it. "At least you're not like to end up in a workhouse—or waiting in an agency for employment and meeting up with the likes of Sallie."

"An *agency?*" he said, sounding so appalled that Molly had to smile. It had been a good thing she had met Sallie after being turned away from Porter and Sons—otherwise, she might have found herself on the street, meeting far less agreeable persons.

"You'd be surprised just how many girls Sallie gets from employment agencies—or from their doorsteps, rather. If you lack references, and I did after the house I'd worked in burnt down, you can't find anything respectable really."

"My God, but you've had the worst run of luck."

Her smiled widened. "Well, the fever in Madras didn't take me. And I didn't drown or shipwreck sailing from India, or burn up in that house fire, so you could say it's better luck than some."

Putting down her wine, she plucked a strawberry from a silver basket and popped it into her mouth. In truth, she knew herself for blessed enough—though it hadn't always seemed so at the time. However, she had seen those hard-painted madams whose girls looked half-starved and half-scared. And she had lived in London long enough to know of the bullies who made their women walk the street.

And just now she was sitting with a gentleman in a fine house.

Yes, if one looked for blessings, there were plenty to find.

Theo kept staring at her, his gaze intense, and she shifted on her pillow, wishing he would make some light quip, or shift with that mercurial mood of his into some other topic. She should not have talked so much about herself.

Glancing around the room, she saw a hobby horse in

the corner and gestured to it. "Was that yours or your brother's?"

Theo glanced at it and then back to her. "Both, in turn. Terrance is five years my senior and outgrew most everything here before I'd come along. And you've strawberry on your lips."

She rubbed at the corner of her mouth, but Theo sat up and brushed his thumb across the other side. Then he took hold of her chin with his thumb and forefinger.

"Is it still there?" she asked, looking up at him as he held her face still.

His expression softened. He nodded. "Still there."

Leaning forward, he touched his lips to the spot his fingers had rubbed. His tongue flickered out, a feathering brush. She let out a breath. Gracious, but it felt so good.

And then he slipped his hand to her waist and leaned forward, pulling her down to the floor with him, and she knew she was on that edge with him again and couldn't afford to let him go further. She wasn't sure she would be able to hold herself back.

Half-turning, she slipped away and struggled to her feet, her face hot and her heartbeat too fast and half of her wishing she could lie back down with him. But she could not risk it. Not when he'd too soon find out that she wasn't the strumpet she pretended. This fantasy was a delicate game. Like the lightest of pastry, it would harden into ruin if handled too much.

From the floor, he glared at her, frustration tight on his face. "Blazes, but you are the worst tease!"

"Tease?" she said, stiffening and not entirely certain what he meant. The gentlemen in Sallie's house used that term often enough, but they said it with an indulgent tone. Theo did not make the word sound an endearment.

"Yes, tease—you torment a man. All tantalizing glimpses and unfulfilled promises!"

"Just what have I promised that I've not given?"

In one fluid move, he rose to his feet. She almost stepped back as he closed on her, but he had a look in his eyes that left her feeling that if she gave ground he'd only start hunting her.

"I've not yet been disinherited—and I'm not going to be at the rate we're going."

"Well, that's hardly my fault, now is it? After all, your father's not a stupid man, and it wouldn't surprise me if he knows this is all a game—folks just know that sort of thing. So don't go blaming me if no one believes that we're not really lovers."

He came a step closer and the heat from him washed over her. Her pulse skidded up a notch faster. Perhaps she should move away, but her feet stuck to the carpet with reluctant muscles that didn't want to step away from him.

Glancing down, he traced a line with his finger from her shoulder, then down the inside of her bare arm to her wrist.

"We'll just have to make the relationship more real then, won't we?"

Mouth dry, she knew she had best dash some cold reality on them both, so she put one hand on her hip and slipped into her best Sallie accent. "I told you—that'll cost more!"

Her words did nothing to extinguish the glittering light in his eyes. *He hasn't drunk that much*, she thought, her pulse skittering now with an answering excitement. *Oh, gracious, perhaps I have!*

"What if I make it an even two hundred pounds for your time with me?"

Lips parting, she stared at him, the shock sizzling through her. "Two hundred," she repeated. He was joking—as she had been the other night. And then she saw how very serious he was.

Molly did the calculation rapidly—if he was offering to round up to two hundred pounds, he must have offered Sallie well over a hundred to start. And she'd once been worried that by taking her fifty pounds she wasn't doing Sallie fair!

Anger began to bubble.

Well, Sallie had said that she had taken her share. What she had omitted was that she'd helped herself to the largest portion.

She pressed her lips tight as the outrage simmered hotter. It wasn't so much the amount—though that sum did dazzle—but the principle of it. Sallie had been willing to let her do all the work.

Well, she'd always known that Sallie had her own code—and here, it seemed, was where she and Sallie parted ways. She would no longer worry about keeping her position at Sallie's house. Besides, with even a hundred pounds in her pocket, she as good as had that inn she wanted.

Only now she had to earn that sum.

Pulling in a breath, she thought about brazenly putting her arms around Theo's neck and pulling him close and giving him his money's worth.

But when it came to actually doing just that, she couldn't move. She couldn't do it. Not for money.

So what did she do?

Well, she was supposed to be a brazen woman, so she said, "Now, ducks, I don't likes to take advantage of you."

His smile crooked and he took her hand to play with her fingers. "But I want to take advantage of you."

Her insides hollowed.

"Come now—two hundred to be my lover. Is that not lure enough?" Theo said, widening his smile. And he could swear he saw hesitation in her glance—and a flicker of desire.

She wet her lips, her tongue darting over the pink softness. He wanted to copy the gesture. But he had the oddest sense that he could frighten her off if he pushed too hard just now. She really wasn't such a jade as she tried to let on, and he wanted with a sudden urgency to take her under his protection.

Then it struck him.

For all the outrageous sums she'd named the other night, she'd been surprised by the amount he had just named. He thought of Sallie insisting on her fifty pounds up front, tucking the money inside her dress—all without Molly in the room.

Sallie must have held out on the girl. What had Sallie named as the sum for her to earn—perhaps only a few pounds? No wonder she'd been so unwilling. And no wonder she'd flippantly named exorbitant sums, for she'd thought he would not pay.

"I've paid Sallie fifty already, but the rest is yours to claim. You've only to be my lover in more than name."

She stared up at him, eyes wide, her lips parted as if to say something—and he knew an opportunity when he saw one.

Catching her waist, he pulled her close and fitted his mouth across hers. She stiffened only for a moment, then loosened into pliant heat. Blazes, but she was ripe for the picking.

He pulled back a moment, then began to feather kisses across the freckles on her nose. Her lashes had lowered, half-veiling the fire in those desire-clouded green eyes.

Two hundred pounds for her—was he mad? That left his pockets empty, but still he could not think it a poor bargain.

Bending over her, he nuzzled her neck just under where the pearl dangled.

A sigh of pure pleasure slipped from her.

He smiled. Once this farce ended, he'd set her up as his mistress proper, and he'd. . . .

Frowning, his kisses stopped and he stood there with

his luscious armful, his mouth still pressed to her skin and his thoughts tripping over themselves.

What was he thinking? He'd never wanted anything but a bit of fun with a woman. Didn't Terrance always say that. . . .

He stopped himself there again.

Who cared what Terrance thought or said? Oh, perhaps once he had looked to have a life like his brother's—careless of what others thought, no ties, no permanence. That seemed to get Terrance only trouble and more trouble. And would it not be a treat to have his Molly snug in some rooms somewhere, just for him.

The idea tugged a smile from him.

But how do I keep her as my mistress if I've no money?

Pulling back from her, he glared at her.

It wasn't her fault that she tempted so. He ached for her. And he could have her. For now. That should be enough.

Only what if one taste of her gave him an appetite for more?

His frown tightened. Of all the times to discover that he had not thought ahead far enough in this! Which meant that he had best figure a way forward through these briars before he tangled himself utterly.

Pushing her away, he held her at arm's length. Her eyes fluttered wide and she stared at him, looking surprised. He nearly pulled her back into his hold, but that was courting too much temptation. No, he had to sort this out with a clear head, and he couldn't do that with her befuddling his senses.

He flicked a finger across her nose. "You're a sweet Sweet, my Molly. Now why don't you go parade those pearls before my father?"

She stared at him a moment, looking as if she might protest, then she frowned and said, "I suppose that is what you're paying me for."

The words cut, and he wanted to protest that he wasn't paying for that. Only he was.

She started for the door, but paused to glance back, confusion in her eyes. He offered back a smile.

You're no more confused than I, my Molly.

An answering smile slowly curved her lips, and then, thank heavens, she left before she tempted him into changing his mind and dragging her into his arms.

Letting out a breath, he ran his fingers through his hair. So what must he do now? He'd bought her—and he had her. Was he best off not to acquire a taste for sweets—or to find a way to keep her?

He wandered to the window and looked out. Bits of blue showed from behind the gray as clouds scudded fast across the sky.

How did a fellow keep a mistress if he had no coins in his pocket or jewels of his own to offer?

He'd had vague ideas before this of keeping himself with the gambling tables, but could he win enough to hold onto his Molly? There was always Europe to travel now with the war ended, with its cheap lodgings and meals. Only he didn't fancy living in some foreign country for the rest of his life.

Oh, damn Terrance.

Perhaps he ought to give Molly his mother's pearls— only, really, he knew that they had to go to Terrance's bride. As did the estate. And that ring and bracelet really had to go back to Smyth and Garson—though maybe he could convince Terrance, once he was re-inherited, that he now owed a debt to his brother.

That thought deepened his frown.

Here he was doing all this for Terrance and he had not so much as heard a word from his brother. Typical! Blazes, but he wished the fellow would show his face so they could all have this out in a good argument that would clear the air.

Turning from the window, he glanced at the remains of the picnic and his frown softened.

Lord, but didn't his sweet Sweet enjoy her meal—along with everything else in life. She had not actually eaten much, but she'd sampled everything—a bite of each to pick her favorites, he had teased last night. However, she had found something to praise in everything. He smiled.

She made the world as bright as that hair of hers. She even thought herself lucky for ending up with Sallie.

Striding from the room, he thought back to that story of her growing up in India, with that uncle of hers. Had she been taken in by some military man? Or had he been a blood relative? She had said her father had been posted to the army. A Captain wasn't it? And wasn't there some book in the house somewhere that listed officers? It might not hurt to glance through the lists and see if the name Sweet came up anywhere, just to see if this was fantasy or truth.

How, after all, did anyone leave a child abandoned on the London docks? Had they not wanted anything to do with the daughter of a cast-off daughter?

One thing he knew—if he ever found a trace of them, it would be difficult to keep from taking after the lot of them with a horsewhip.

And all of this is just my way of not looking at this puzzle I now have—for it's going to be damn difficult to both keep my Molly, and keep away from her enough, until I see a clear path for us here.

Molly came downstairs for dinner dressed and ready to play her part, and muttering "two hundred" under her breath over and over to remember what he had really offered to pay her. She had to in order to keep thinking about that and not how her lips still tingled from Theo's kiss.

She was not doing this well. But she would do better tonight to act a bought woman, for she was one proper now. Theo had sent her a slim coin purse with shillings and crowns that came out to around ten pound, with a note carried to her on a silver tray by one of the footmen.

On account.

Two words and payment made. She had the money tucked away, and an obligation before her to help him get thrown out of the house. So she wore all the jewels—pearls, diamonds, and the emerald—and the peacock-blue dress. She hadn't been able to find the squire earlier to parade the pearls before him. And she hadn't looked that hard. Her stomach still quivered at the thought of how he might react.

But she had to act like a hard woman who didn't care.

What she found was that she blushed too easily when Theo smiled at her and greeted her, and she fussed with the diamond bracelet around her wrist, and she wanted to steal glances at him when he wasn't looking so that she would remember forever how handsome he looked.

None of it seemed to her what a jade of a woman would do.

And she alternated between panic at what she might have to do for her hundred and fifty pounds, and the hot rush of desire at just such thoughts.

Which just shows how poor a business woman I really am, she thought. Even though she still could summon some anger at Sallie, she also had to admire how the woman could put herself first above all else. That was a real talent.

For all her worry, however, the squire hardly glanced at the pearls and said nothing about them. She looked at Theo, sending him a silent question as to what she should do now, but he stared absently into his wine glass, hardly noticing himself.

There was little conversation at dinner, unless she made it. The squire's dogs seemed, in fact, to be the only ones listening to her, and they were actually more interested to see what she might slip them from the table.

Afterwards, she played backgammon with Theo, beating him easily in two games. Theo claimed that the squire standing over him—and therefore the dogs clustered about his legs—in the second game had caused his loss.

The squire only snorted, then said, "You've no head for the game—never did have the patience. Now, your mother—"

He broke off the words with a glance at the pearls around Molly's neck. Face hot, she almost put a hand up to touch them.

When the squire turned away and started for the brandy, Molly found the words slipping out, "I suppose you think you could best me, d'you, ducks?"

Thirteen

She wanted to lure him away from the shadows in the room, and those in himself. The poor man needed some distraction. And so she ignored Theo's hot stare on her and the dogs' heavy panting breath.

The squire glanced at her, his bushy black eyebrows lowered, his expression unreadable. Then he shuffled Theo from his seat, telling him to watch how it was done as he settled into his chair with his dogs about him.

For the first part of the game, Molly was too aware of Theo hovering beside her, his irritation almost swamping her senses. The dogs milled under the table, brushing against her legs, almost as if they, too, did not like being left out of things. But then the counters began piling up on the squire's side, and she focused on the game. She would not have anyone thinking she ever gave anything but her best—even for just a game.

She won—but only by a lucky toss of the dice that got her last pieces home first. The squire bested her on the next game, issuing a crow of delight that set his dogs to barking as well.

Then she realized that Theo was glowering at her, and this was doing nothing to help him become disinherited, so she bowed out from another challenge. She took herself off to bed and, as she did, she heard the squire stopping Theo from following her with some question about the estate.

They went on like that on the following day as well. *A game we're all playing*, she thought. But could any of them actually win?

Theo got her onto a horse the day after, saying that it was time she learned to ride. She protested, but when he threatened to simply pick her up and put her onto the nearest mount he could find in the stable, she gave in to him. Dressed in her most durable gown, she allowed him to lead her around the stables at a walk and then a bouncing trot. She kept thinking it a very long way to the ground, particularly since there was no side saddle in the stable and she sat sideways on Theo's saddle, clutching the horse's mane with one hand and the back of the saddle with the other.

However, she stayed on and found herself pleased to have succeeded and to actually be interested in improving her skills.

As she slipped from the saddle, into Theo's waiting arms, he grinned at her. "We'll have you jumping tomorrow."

She slanted him a look. Then became aware of just how broad his shoulders were under her palms and of how his hands spanned her waist. His smile stilled and her lips parted. Would he kiss her, even with the grooms watching?

Only then the squire strode into the yard, demanding, "Theo, I want a word with you!"

She tensed. Had the squire's patience snapped at last? Theo glanced at his father, the corner of his mouth crooked and a gleam of satisfaction in his eyes. "About what, sir?"

"Sheep—we've the shearing schedule to set for the autumn."

Theo's mouth thinned, and Molly almost laughed. Would they never offend the squire enough?

As if to goad his father, Theo slid his arm even more

firmly—and possessively—around her waist. "I'm spending the afternoon with Molly."

The squire frowned. "If you're marrying the chit, you'll have your life with her. So you can attend to me today."

For a moment, Theo's arm tensed, and Molly wasn't certain what he would do. But then he glanced down at her and his expression softened. "Oh, there's never enough time with my Molly. Besides, I've a promise to keep for you, do I not?"

Mind blank, she stared up at him. And then she wanted to kick him for putting it all onto her to come up with an excuse for them. The mischief lurking in those blue eyes drove her to come up with a suitable revenge.

Smiling, she said, her tone vulgarly low, "That's right, ducks. You're taking me to Lady Thorpe's for that visit I said as I'd make—just fancy me bein' neighbors with a real ladyship these days!"

"Why in blazes did you think up this as an excuse for us?" Theo grumbled, setting the horses to a lively trot. Burke had returned to Winslow Park yesterday, leading Terrance's matched bay horses, both now sound. So Theo had decided to take them out today and drive his brother's curricle.

She glanced at him. They were traveling to Lady Thorpe's in style, with a summer sky overhead and the breeze snapping the hem of her green and yellow striped gown. In the sunlight, her diamond bracelet was enough to blind.

"It's as good as any," she said, her tone reasonable. "Besides, your father didn't look any too pleased about you parading me around to your neighbors."

He grimaced. "You could have said I'd be in your bed."

Her cheeks warmed, but she turned to watch sheep

graze a green field. Winslow sheep, she assumed. "That wouldn't have put that look on your face, now would it?"

"What look?"

"The same one you had when you talked of all those eels you ate. Next time, Mr. Winslow, you may invent your own tale if you want one to suit your fancy."

"Next time, Miss Sweet, I'll simply throw you over my shoulder and carry you off under my father's nose."

She glanced up at him. For all his bold talk now, he had done little in the past two days to lay any claim on her. That puzzled her. Had it been the chase he wanted, not the prize? But, if so, why did she still feel this . . . this sizzle of . . . of something crackling between them?

And she had no idea what to do about it. Questions might only bring answers she did not want to hear. So she would wait and see. But she rather wished he was back to chasing after her for a kiss, or an intimate touch, or a bit more.

So much for my high morals, she thought. It was probably best, anyway, they had not been tempted further.

He grumbled the rest of the way to Lady Thorpe's. But Molly was pleased that his presence forced Lady Thorpe's butler into a respectful welcome. They found her ladyship in the rose garden with Sylvain Harwood.

Theo brightened at that. "Hello, Silly," he said, sounding more like a brother to her. "What sort of animal have you got with you today? Something we can eat I hope."

The girl seemed not to mind this nickname, but she made a face at his teasing. Then she had to introduce them to Lady Thorpe, for her ladyship showed no memory of having met Molly and expressed surprise that Theo had grown so much. She did not mistake either of them for anyone from her past, however.

"It's one of her better days," Sylvain explained, leaning closer to Molly.

It was, but it showed all the more what a tragedy it was

that this lovely woman seemed to be losing herself. At least she had the past to hold, Molly thought, for her ladyship seemed able to recall the events of decades ago with ease even if she could not remember last week.

So Molly encouraged her to tell of how she had been courted by her late husband—a man with a reputation as a fortune hunter and gambler, who had not been approved by her family.

"We ran off to Gretna, and he was so disappointed that no one chased us," her ladyship said, a smile dancing in her eyes. "But I think they had already done with that over Amy."

"Your sister?" Molly asked, unable to stop a quickening of interest.

Lady Thorpe smiled, then unfastened a locket pin from the white lace shawl around her shoulders. Opening it, she showed the tiny portraits to Molly. "That's my dear Thorpe on the right and my sister on the left. She married an army man—a nobody—and my parents never forgave her. And I never forgave them for coming between us."

Eagerly, Molly glanced at the locket. Surely there were too many similarities in circumstance—Amy and Amelia. Both women marrying into the army. Both at odds with their family. There had to be some connection. Yet, as she stared at the painted face in the small oval, her hopes splintered like a basket made of spun sugar dropped onto a stone floor.

The blonde girl with the somber face was nothing like what she remembered of her mother, who had had dark hair and had always smiled and laughed and sang.

There was no connection to recognize. And that was the danger of living too much in fantasy. It hurt so very much when it was revealed as false.

Handing back the locket, she busied herself by asking for more tea, and then turned to talk to Sylvain.

Theo watched Molly's reaction to the locket, frowning. Nothing ever troubled her, so why did she seem bothered now? She was smiling still, only those green eyes of hers did not gleam with humor. He frowned at Lady Thorpe as she refastened her locket—and then he remembered how Molly had reacted to being mistaken for Lady Thorpe's niece. Blazes, but she still wanted to be related to this mad old lady?

He frowned, thinking of Molly's stories of her early years. He had not looked very long for the book in the house with army records, and now he wished he had kept at it. It would have been nice to give Molly something—something she could keep, not some bit of jewelry that he must take back, but something she might really value. Even if it was just the sight of her father's name in a book.

He wanted, he realized, to have her smile at him with that utter delight in her eyes as she had had when she'd first glimpsed the picnic.

Only now she was bothered, and so was he.

Blazes, but he had known it as a poor idea to come on this visit and he'd been proven right.

He waited a quarter hour, then started hinting that they must go. But Lady Thorpe kept remembering yet another story of her sister or her late husband, or someone else dead.

It was more than grim.

Sylvain seemed not the least upset by this, but then he had always thought she had more in common with her wild beasts than any civilized soul. However, Molly listened to the stories with a wistful look in her eyes that just about tore a fellow open.

Finally, he managed to pry Molly loose.

He took her to Halsage. A walk about the village and a stop at The Four Feathers would be a treat. But he found himself too aware of the stares and whispers following them, and he came near to knocking down George Afton in the inn when the man started winking and leering at Molly, as if she were some common strumpet.

Which she wasn't. Not really. Or, at least, well, she might be a strumpet and of common blood, but she was quite out of the ordinary in every other way.

So he took her arm and led her back to Terrance's curricle and contented himself with driving her around the neighborhood, pointing out the sights he could name and making up names for the rest of it.

That evening, after changing for dinner and doing himself up just for her in a black evening coat, a proper cravat, and a gold brocade waistcoat, he did his best to keep her attention on himself. And he ignored his father glowering at them. He also refused his father's demand that he spend time after dinner talking over more estate business.

"If you want to talk sheep, get Terrance to come home!" he burst out at the end of the evening. Then he strode off to his own rooms, angry with his father for pushing at him, with Terrance for not being there to deal with it, and with himself for losing his temper.

The squire stared after his youngest son, just as angry. The insolent pup! Talking to his father in that tone! Gads, but he'd. . . .

He'd what? Disinherit him? He had done that with one son and it had done nothing to amend the lad's behavior.

Stalking into his study, the squire slammed the door behind him. He then had to open it again as indignant and insistent paw scratches sounded on the door. The dogs piled in through the open door, tails waving as each made for a favored spot. Then the squire strode to the brandy decanter.

When he had a full glass in his hand, he stared at the amber liquid, swirling it, letting the strong, acidic fumes fill his nostrils and his senses.

He had thought this madness between Theo and

that . . . that girl to be nothing. But he could see the intimacy blossoming between them. The two of them spoke without words, sharing looks and touches that told of more than an infatuation.

In little more than a fortnight, the banns would have been called and Theo could marry the girl.

The squire frowned.

He'd as good as given his blessing, but that had been when he was certain the lad would not go through with it. However, he had gone into Halsage that morning and had heard the muffled snickers behind his back. Theo Winslow marrying a London strumpet—like to like, he'd heard the mutters.

Well, he would not see the Winslow name ridiculed.

He tossed back his brandy. He'd throw the girl out, by gads! Have her tossed out with those outrageous dresses of hers. Tonight. He glanced out the darkened windows. Well, perhaps tomorrow. At first light. Yes, that would do!

He poured himself another brandy. Then he thought how he had proclaimed her impertinent one morning. She had thanked him for it as if she had not known the meaning of the word. But she had. He had seen it in her eyes.

Little baggage!

She never seemed to fear crossing swords over coffee. A smile tugged his mouth and he wiped it away with a deep swallow of brandy.

Well, perhaps he'd have her thrown out after breakfast.

Yes, give her one more go round, for it wouldn't do to have her thinking she had ever got the best of him. Yes, after breakfast would do far better than at first light.

But then she came downstairs the next morning in breeches.

He nearly dropped his coffee cup. They looked to be Theo's old clothes—breeches, riding boots, a billowing white shirt too large for her, and a riding coat as well. She only lacked a cravat and waistcoat to look a man—except there was nothing masculine about that figure of hers.

Tightening his grip on the china, he ignored the coffee that had sloshed out of his cup onto the table, and demanded, "What in blazes are you dressed indecent for?"

As he raised his voice, the dogs' nails clattered on the wood as they skittered under the table.

She put a hand on her hip and stared back at him. "If a gent can wear breeches and have it seem decent, then that's decent enough for me. Besides, Theo wants me to jump today and if I'm to ride astride it's this or nothing and I think horse hair would itch me bare arse."

He almost burst out with a laugh and had to change it to a cough. Then he scowled at her. Gads, but she looked even younger today than ever.

And then she was frowning at him and moving to the sideboard to fill a plate. "You've not eaten again this morning, and you smell of stale brandy! No wonder you're so cross. And here's Mrs. Brown making the best buttered eggs."

"I'm not hungry!" he snapped.

"Yes, you are. It's why you're so disagreeable in the mornings."

"That's a fancy word for the likes of you."

She grinned. "Ain't it just, ducks. Now start on that, if you can. I'm going to fetch you somethin' I used to make for my uncle's head on one of his late mornings."

He started to tell her she was impertinent, but he had said that before, and she was gone already from the room. He pushed the plate away. The smell of warm eggs and bacon tempted a little, but it also set his stomach turning.

He put a hand on it. His head did ache, and his insides churned sour from too much brandy.

A moment later she returned and put a pewter mug in front of him.

He glared at the white froth. "What's that?"

"A panda—rum, sugar, butter, nutmeg, and lemon."

He pushed it away. "Bah! Sick room food for an invalid."

"Yes, and a sick room is just where you'll be if you don't care for yourself. Drinking too much, and not eating! Your dogs get better than you give yourself! But drink it or throw it out as suits you! I've a horse to ride."

With that she strode from the room, stopping only long enough to take a bite of bacon with her.

He glanced at the mug again, his stomach turning. Then he picked it up, sniffed it and drained it. It went down sweet and tasty—and after a few moments, settled his insides like a blessing.

Blast the girl for being right.

He glared at the door a moment, then glanced at the rapidly cooling bacon and eggs. Mrs. Brown did indeed make up a good set of buttered eggs—fluffy things. Pulling the plate close, he began to eat. From under the table, one of the dogs nudged his knee.

But this wasn't due to anything she'd said, he told himself. No, he was just hungry.

That evening he watched her play backgammon with his son as Plato rested his head on his knee. He glared at them, but they paid no heed, and so he picked up the latest edition of *The Sporting Magazine* and opened it.

Theo was teasing her about nearly coming unseated in trotting over no more than a fallen branch, and she kept laughing at his jokes and promising revenge upon him in the game. And finally, to keep from wandering over to join them, he got up and strode out, his dogs at his heels.

Instead of going to his study, he did something he had not done in years.

He went to Julia's room.

With a candlestick in one hand, he stepped into the room. He shut the dogs out, and left them to scratch on the door, though they soon stopped.

The cold of the place wrapped around him—and the

faint scent of roses. He almost turned and walked out, but that would make him a coward. He wasn't that. So, mouth set, he stiffened and stepped forward.

Her portrait still hung here. He'd never been able to bring himself to order it taken down—or have this room made over. He ought to have. Ought to have ordered everything sold, or put up in the attic, or burned. But he could not let go of it. Not a stick of it. Nor an ounce of her.

Oh, Julia!

He stared up at the painting now, the pain twisting in his heart as it had almost twenty years ago. Tall, slim, graceful, black-haired, with eyes the color of fine sherry. Terrance looked so like her. But this Molly of Theo's seemed a different creature entirely.

Only the laughter was the same—bright as a candle.

He glared at the portrait.

Candles burned out. Or could be snuffed. He knew how to do that.

Turning on his heel, he strode out, shutting the door behind him as if that could shut away his past. His regrets.

He'd throw that girl out of the house tomorrow. By gads, he would. He'd not let any son of his make the same mistakes he had with a wrong marriage.

But he didn't order her gone.

He tried—gads, he tried. Only, just as with that blasted room of Julia's, he could not bring himself to give the orders he knew he should. He despised himself for that weakness. And that made him desperate.

Desperate enough to swallow enough of his pride to take up a pen and write a letter that would put an end to this farce.

And he kept telling himself that it was all for Theo's good.

But was it?

* * *

"You're not supposed to like him, and you're supposed to have him dislike you! But just look at you—do you call that scandalous? You'll have to leave off your shift and go about looking more a strumpet and less like a girl trying to be proper!"

Shoulders squared back, Molly stared at her reflection. Her lecture to herself wasn't taking.

She had tried on the thin yellow muslin gown with and without a shift. She ought to wear it without—you could see straight through the muslin.

She could not do it.

"A fine harlot you make," she said, glaring at herself.

It was no use. If she went downstairs without her shift on, her blushes would betray her, and so she'd be best off to wear it. At least her shift ended mid-thigh so the muslin would show her legs. But her wearing breeches hadn't done the trick with the squire, either.

Theo had sworn it would.

But Theo knew little enough about his father, it seemed, and the squire knew even less about his son. Oh, these Winslow men! Hard heads, and no sense in them. If only she could put the two of them in a room and make them talk to each other.

However, she suspected that they'd turn their backs to each other and pretend the other one wasn't there. That seemed to be how a Winslow dealt with something he did not want to notice.

"And how am I ever going to earn my money at this rate?" she muttered. However, it wasn't her hundred and fifty pounds—well, hundred and forty now—that she thought about as she lay in bed at night. It was how good Theo's arms felt around her, and how much she enjoyed her evenings with him.

And how could she sort out this matter between Theo and his father?

In the past week, the more time she spent with the

squire the more she found herself seeing a lonely old man, afraid for his son's future. A man who hated to say he'd ever made a mistake. And a father worried for his son. She longed to tell him she didn't mean Theo anything but good.

But she would also have to tell him about Theo's worries over his brother's inheritance. And she doubted the squire would have much admiration for Theo's plan.

Oh, but Theo really should not be courting his father's wrath. Only look what bitterness such rows had left as a legacy for Lady Thorpe's family—and even in her own. She didn't want more "if onlys" for Theo.

Still, she had to remember that the squire was a man who had disowned his eldest. He was flint-hearted, and Theo was best away from that. But she'd started to think that flint in him ran about as deep as paper. Mrs. Brown had certainly seemed to think that if the squire's eldest came home to be raged at the entire matter might then be considered settled by the squire.

Only Terrance, it seemed, was even less likely to obey his father than was Theo.

Well, at least she no longer worried about this taking so long. She had reason enough to give Sallie her notice when she got back to London. And she hoped to do so with the money for her inn in her pocket. Yes, that was the true brightness behind the clouds of worry. Just like the sky that day.

Despite the day starting warm, by mid-morning the weather looked uncertain. Clouds piled in the west, tumbling into each other and turning dark with rain. The pending storm left the air still and heavy, and left Molly restless.

Theo had wanted her to go riding with him that morning. He insisted she was ready for a gallop, but with muscles still aching from their last lesson, she had sent him away, telling him she wanted to ready herself for that promised trip to the Norman Tower. Only now she rather thought she might try to lure him into billiards instead.

Or perhaps into visiting Lady Thorpe. That would be dry enough if they took a closed carriage.

She had gone once on her own to visit Lady Thorpe. Sylvain had been there again—and was introduced as the Duchess of York. She had then become Lady Thorpe's lost niece, and while it had unsettled her at first, she soon discovered she enjoyed being someone's relative. A relief that, since the Winslows were enough to make anyone wonder about the pleasures of having blood kin.

A half hour later, and after more almond cakes than she could count, she had found herself quite at home.

It seemed, too, as if Lady Thorpe's too protective butler, Grieg, had decided she intended no harm. Or perhaps he trusted Sylvain to keep an eye on her. In either case, he had been almost pleasant.

But going to Lady Thorpe's was like stepping into a dream. And a body always had to wake up. At least she knew that. Only she didn't think that knowledge would really give her feelings any protection.

With a shake of her head, she went downstairs.

The squire, however, was not there to scandalize with the thin muslin. That left her rather put out—all that effort and only Simpson, two of the maids, and a footman whose eyes grew large as she walked past him to impress with her wicked ways.

Perhaps she ought to have taken Theo up on his suggestions to ride in the altogether.

Going off to the billiards room, she practiced her shots and she kept watching the drive for Theo's return.

She had no idea which horse he had taken from the stable. In truth, she actually had a difficult time telling one from another, unless they happened to be different colors. But she would never admit that to Theo. He seemed to regard each horse as a close friend. Much as did the squire. They were alike in that, as in so many ways.

Her shot went wide, but she did not even take note, for ideas had begun to spin.

So alike—and she certainly knew Theo's weakness. He had shown it the first day they met in how he had reacted to her calling him a boy. It would be the same with his father. Gracious, this had been there before her all along. Only she had not wanted to see it—had not wanted to recognize the truth of it.

It would work. But afterwards Theo might well not want anything more to do with her. Still, she had to tell him. And he might feel better about everything, too, if it got him what he wanted. So all might yet be well.

Thunder grumbled and she glanced out the windows to glimpse a horseman galloping towards the house with reckless ease.

It had to be Theo.

Putting away her billiards stick, she headed towards the stable, her heart beating fast as she tried to sort out the exact way to tell him. She would start first with the news that she had exactly the plan that would work, and then she'd tell him the rest.

And she tried not to think about how this also meant the end of her time at Winslow Park, and with him.

But perhaps, later, he would come help her with her inn? After all, he would have nothing else to do.

And perhaps I might as well wish for wings.

Hurrying her steps, she ran outside, her skirts lifted.

She had forgotten about her scandalous dress until she stepped into the stable-yard and the groom stopped in the act of leading a puffing gray horse into the stables.

"Theo, I've just the—"

She broke off the words as the gentleman turned and she realized that it wasn't Theo, but a taller, broader version of him. He wore his hat at the same rakish angle. But his eyes were tawny brown, not blue.

"You're not Theo!"

Fourteen

As soon as the words slipped out, she knew how stupid
they sounded. But she had not been able to keep the disappointment within. Not Theo—Terrance.

He grinned at her, an uncannily similar expression to
Theo's. "Perceptive of you. However, you certainly must
be his fancy piece—and I can see why he took you up."

Her cheeks warmed but there was little she could do
about the thin muslin of her gown. He was staring at her,
his gaze assessing, and as thunder rumbled in the distance she gave him back just as much measuring.

A brown riding coat hung open, showing a buff waistcoat stretched over a broad chest. Black riding boots and
buckskin breeches shaped muscular legs, looking as expensive as only clothes made to a perfect fit could.
Instead of a white cravat, he wore a white-dotted blue
kerchief knotted at his neck.

He had the look of a Winslow in his square jaw and
straight nose. With his glittering eyes and reddened
cheeks, he also looked a bit drunk, though he stood
steady on his feet.

"As a prodigal son, you leave a fair bit to be desired,"
she said, already cross with him. He looked a care-for-
nobody, and she could box his ears for all the trouble he
had caused his brother and father.

Black eyebrows lifted for a moment with affronted irritation, but then amusement glimmered in his eyes.

In two strides, he crossed the distance to her and his large hands wrapped tight around her waist. By instinct, she stiffened and pushed against him. She might as well have pushed against the stone wall around the stable yard.

He only smiled more. "If we're talking of what's desired, let's speak more of you, my little bird of paradise."

Fat, wet drops—too few yet to be called rain—began to splatter on them and around them. But he took no notice.

She glared up at him. "I'd rather go inside and avoid both a wetting and you!"

He gave a laugh.

He was taller and broader than Theo—coarser-made. His features, while handsome, lacked the refinement of Theo's, and dissipation had left its mark as well, roughening his skin and the edges of his jaw and cheeks, like the blunting of a knife.

But a blunt knife still could cut, she knew.

He pulled her closer and she leaned back, though her waist now pressed against him. "There's just no avoiding some things in life."

She pushed again, but it did no good. He smelled of ale and brandy, and every instinct warned against him. This time she saw the jagged lightning as it flashed in the sky. Seconds later, thunder rumbled.

Worried, she glanced up at the sky, then at him. "And other things are easily avoided. We're about to be soaked."

He paid no heed, but only said, "I couldn't believe the story in London that m'brother had been seen leaving town with a fancy piece. The question is, while it's obvious what he's doing with you, why in hades is he doing it here in the ancestral pile?"

She almost blurted out the truth—that it was all his fault. However, it really ought to be Theo who told him. So she broadened her Sallie voice, saying, "He brought me home to marry me, he did. And he won't be none too happy to hear you've been handlin' me!"

He grinned again and she saw he had wolfish teeth, with points edging two of them. Her stomach knotted. If it had been Terrance come to Sallie's for a woman, Molly would have turned him away on first sight.

"If I'm to be your brother-in-law, seems only fair that I kiss the bride."

He started to pull her to him, but she put her hand up, knocking off his hat, before she managed to cover her mouth. Then she said, the words muffled by her fingers, "Kisses come after the marriage, ducks!"

Capturing her wrist, he dragged it behind her. "Not in my books—'ducks.'"

She twisted again, but he had hold of her other wrist and swept her arms behind her. Then he turned her so her back pressed against the stone of the stable yard wall. Wet drops splashed to the ground around them and onto her face like angry tears.

"Here now—what sort of gentlemen do you call yourself!"

"Not much of one at all," he said, his tone pleasant. And then he leaned toward her.

Clenching her back teeth, she made up her mind to bite him, but in the next moment there was a clatter almost as loud as thunder of steel-shod hooves on the cobbled yard.

Terrance's hold on her loosened as he half turned at the interruption, and in the next instant, he spun away from her as if dragged.

She looked up to see Theo already off his horse, one hand fisted into his brother's coat lapels and blue eyes blazing as his fist connected with his brother's jaw in a cracking sound that made her wince.

Terrance staggered back, his heel slipping on the wet cobbles. He went down with a grunt.

Standing over his brother, Theo shook the pain from

the knuckles of his right hand. "Blazes, but you always did have a head thick as oak!"

Starting to sit up, Terrance rubbed his jaw. "That was a lucky punch."

"Get up and I'll show you lucky," Theo said, settling into a boxing stance. His brother carried an extra four stone on him, but he had the advantage of speed. He'd have to use it to keep away from his brother's left, for the man had a wicked reach.

Terrance grinned and stood, but before they could square off, Molly had hold of Theo's arm, dragging it down, forcing him to glance at her.

When he'd ridden into the yard, he'd only seen her tousled red hair and his brother's back—fury blurred the rest into a haze. And then he'd been off his horse and dragging Terrance off Molly.

Anger with his brother still boiled in him, but the pain in his hand from the blow he'd struck had shocked him from that haze. Now he glanced at Molly, at her hair, damp and curling, and at how her gown clung to her form, transparent, showing her breasts and waist and curving legs.

His scowl deepened and he wanted to hit Terrance again—blazes, but what was his brother doing, poaching on another man's turf!

"Please, stop this," Molly begged.

He almost shook her off. Instead, he glared at his brother. Terrance was trying to strip off his riding coat, cursing at its tight fit, and had managed to get the shoulders down. It tempted Theo to take a crack at him now. Not very sporting, but how satisfying to knock him down again.

"Oh, for. . . ." he started to say, then glanced at Molly again and at the grooms gathering in the yard—one of them had hold of his horse—and he straightened.

"You'd best come inside," he said, speaking both to Molly and Terrance.

"Damn if I will!" Terrance said, still struggling with his coat. "You there, give a hand," he told a groom. The fellow grabbed hold of the sleeves and dragged, pulling the jacket off.

Terrance squared off at once against his brother. "Come on now—let's see if your luck holds."

Irritation with his brother welled in Theo—years of it, he realized. Where had Terrance ever been when he'd wanted him around? He'd followed after Terrance, copied him, tried to be him, in fact. And all it'd ever gotten him was—nothing. Eyes narrowing, Theo realized that he had never wanted anything so much as to wipe the smirk from his brother's face just now.

He wanted to pound some sense into the bounder, damn it.

Taking Molly's hands, he put her away from him. Then he shrugged out of his own loose-fit coat and handed it to her. "Won't be but a minute."

Molly glanced from Theo to his brother. Terrance looked even larger without his coat on. His shirt sleeves billowed, fluttering in the breeze. Rain spattered down on all of them, and she wished the clouds would loosen a torrent that might stop this. But the drops continued to fall in splatters.

She looked again at Theo, now in his shirtsleeves. He had his fists up and looked ready to move light on the balls of his feet. But she could not allow this. Not a fight of brother against brother.

"Stop it!" she said, striding between them, clutching Theo's jacket. "Stop this."

Theo glanced at her, blue eyes sharp and pale. "Stand aside. This is about you—and far more than that!"

"I don't care what it's about. I don't want anyone hurt—and I don't want you hurting your brother."

Terrance gave a laugh. "He won't do that—though I promise only to blacken both his eyes."

She rounded on him. "For what? For making you feel foolish because you were acting a fool? You're a bully, just like your father tries to be, and you ought to be looking after your brother, not trying to hit him!"

Turning, she glared at Theo. "And you—oh, you've got to stop."

Jaw set, he glared at her. "Step aside, Molly. I won't have him handling you like that."

Terrance straightened and let his hands drop. "Bloody hell, this isn't about how I handle your strumpet, it's—"

"I'm not his strumpet. I'm not anyone's strumpet. I'm a cook in a bawdy house, and no one is going to fight over me or for me or in front of me!" Molly stamped her foot on the cobblestones and both men turned to stare at her, eyes wide and mouths open.

Embarrassment scorched her face as she realized what she had just said. Then she drew in a breath and let it out. Well, Theo now knew the worst of her, but she found she couldn't meet his eyes to see his reaction to this. At least she seemed to have stopped their fighting.

Turning on her heel, she strode to the house. Thunder cracked behind her and the rain began to pour down, so she had that excuse to break into a run. And she could always tell herself, too, that the thunder had drowned out Theo's calling her name rather than that he had not called after her at all.

"Quite the spitfire," Terrance said. He wiped the rain from his face. Then he glanced around and held out his hand for his coat. His anger had faded and he no longer wanted to give back his brother two punches for the lucky one that had landed him flat.

Theo turned to him, eyes glassy.

"You need a drink," Terrance said, laying an arm across his brother's shoulders. "And to unburden your soul—what in hades are you doing bringing a cook home as your doxy?"

"A cook," Theo repeated, his tone hollow.

Terrance glanced at his brother.

He had been drinking steadily on his journey home—mostly in anticipation of having to see his father. He always handled that better drunk, for then he didn't give a damn about the squire's disapproval or the inevitable arguments. But he'd been unable to resist the lure of coming home—it was just too tempting that he might glimpse Theo flaunting his mistress before their father. But nothing seemed to be what he'd expected. The mistress was not a proper mistress at all, but a cook. And there was this story of Theo wanting to marry her—what was that about?

"Come and tell me all," he ordered.

After ordering brandy from the grim, disapproving Simpson, Terrance took his brother up to his rooms. It was a safe enough haven, for their father always demanded their attendance in a public room, and would never stoop so low as to hunt them down in their own holes. It also gave Terrance a chance to change his wet, dirty clothes—he now stank like a horse, he thought.

As he stripped bare, washed, and changed into dry clothes, he also extracted the story from Theo, dragging it out with question after question.

"So you see, it's all your fault!" Theo said, finally, glaring at his brother. He turned the glass of brandy in his hands. *A cook! A cook, of all things!*

Terrance's head reappeared from the shirt he was donning. "And how do you figure your stuffing your nose into my business to be my fault? Did I ask you to step in?"

"Well, I'm not going to take your inheritance—did you ever think about what a bind you put me in, leaving it all to me to deal with father?" Theo asked, glaring at his brother. He put down his brandy glass.

Terrance glared back. "I ought to have darkened your daylights when I had the chance—curse it, just leave father to me."

"So you can avoid him better than I? You never come home, not unless you're foxed, overspent on your allowance, or need a repairing lease. And so I'm the one father uses to rant about your behavior. I'm also the one he tries to talk to about sheep and shearing and acres to plant!"

Terrance grinned suddenly. "Sheep?"

"Sheep!" Theo said, his tone disgusted. Then a reluctant smile edged up his mouth. "And if they were mine, I'd be thinking of crossing in some Romneys."

"God save me," Terrance said, and drank back his brandy. "But what will you do about your cook now? If you mean to cast her off, I've—" He broke off at Theo's hot glare, then held up his palms and said, "Just trying to offer brotherly help."

With a rude snort, Theo rose. "Help yourself, you mean. Molly is my lookout here, and I'd best go find her and talk to her."

"She's made for more than talk, brother," Terrance said, his teeth showing.

Theo shot him a glare, then he left the room in search of Molly. She was not in her room, so he started to hunt for her.

A cook!

His mind still could not latch onto that. She was a cook, she had said. Had she said it simply to shock them? She had looked ready to do anything to keep them from fighting. But, blazes, it fit too well—her interest in food and recipes, her blushes, her reluctance to allow what any jade had ready for sale.

What rankled most was that he'd been made into a

buffoon by her and Sallie. Duped by them. Had they laughed at how Theo Winslow couldn't tell the difference between a woman of experience and a woman with none? That festered like a sore.

Frowning, he strode into the library.

He found her there, seated at a writing desk, paper in front of her. She stood at once.

She had changed into that striped dress that she had first worn, and seeing it deepened his scowl. It made him remember her coming down the stairs with Sallie. Smiling.

Laughing at him, no doubt.

He glared at her. "Is it true?"

She looked up from the carpet, and he had to fold his arms and tighten the furrow in his brow to keep from giving in to those wide green eyes. But the look in her eyes was all the answer he needed.

"You're a better actress than I thought!" he said, his tone sharp and intending to wound.

She looked away, then glanced up again and gestured to the desk behind her. "I've left the bracelet and ring in the drawer with your mother's pearls. I . . . I don't know if I should thank you for knocking down your brother, but, well, thank you."

He hunched a shoulder. "As a cook, I don't suppose you're accustomed to being mauled like that."

"Oh, for . . . you wanted a low woman—and, actually, I'd finally thought of a way to make your father disinherit you. It was there before me all along, only . . . well, I didn't want to tell you the truth. I didn't want to give up . . . I mean, I thought you might think me . . . I mean, might not pay me. But now you can just tell your father everything and that'll do the trick for you."

"What trick? Tell me everything about what?"

Theo turned to find his father in the doorway. He cursed himself for not shutting the door behind him—and locking it.

The squire came into the room, his dogs at his heels. "Well, d'you have something to tell me?"

Theo glanced at Molly. She had her chin up, but she looked even paler than the paper on the table. What, had she planned to leave here with a note as a good-bye? She could just forget that.

He turned to his father, suddenly unwilling to have Molly's past laid out for the squire to tear into. Instead, he said, "Yes—we wanted to tell you that Terrance is home." Instead of being surprised, the squire nodded and Theo's eyes narrowed. "You expected him, sir?"

The squire glanced at Molly, then turned to Theo and said, his tone belligerent, "'Course I did. I wrote him of your wedding—and that I've decided to forgive him!"

Eyes wide, Molly stared at the squire, then she glanced at Theo. Why hadn't he told his father yet that she was a cook? The question seemed of no importance now, however. The squire had taken his eldest back in, and without Theo having had to get himself thrown out.

It seemed that her use here was done entirely.

And Theo knew she was just a cook. She glanced at him—he had been shocked and wounded, she suspected. Pride—these Winslow men seemed to have pounds of the stuff. She would have done better, she knew now, to have told him at once and to have had him present her as such to his father. That would have done the trick at once, for the squire was as proud a man as his sons.

But here she was in "if onlys" again, and the truth was that she had been enjoying her play-acting far too much. She hadn't wanted Theo to think badly of her. She had wanted to go on pretending to be his mistress.

Now she was nothing to him.

"Forgive him?" Theo said, his voice dull as he repeated his father's word. He snapped his fingers. "Just like that—he's no longer a son, but now he is again. We all dance to your tune, just because you call it on a whim!"

"You're impertinent, lad!"

"I'm bloody fed up, is what I am! How long do we wait until the next time you decide you don't like what we do or how we do it? When is the next time you crack the whip of your good will and approval to make us jump through your hoops!"

The squire's face reddened. "Don't try me, boy!"

"It's about time someone did! Blazes, but you are a bully, just as Molly said."

Turning on Molly, the squire glared at her. "Making trouble, are you, you—"

Theo interrupted, stepping between his father and Molly. "Leave her out of this—this is between us!"

But then a voice from the doorway drawled, "So where does that leave me fitting in?"

Everyone turned to stare at Terrance, who lounged in the doorway now, looking amused.

The squire's frown deepened, Theo glared at his brother and Molly glanced from one Winslow to the other, blinking and lost.

As Terrance strolled into the room, accusations flew, voices rose, interrupting each other, and she watched as the Winslows began to argue in earnest.

The squire's voice finally rose loud enough to cut through the noise, sending the dogs to hide behind the couch. "That's enough! This is my house, by gads, and you're my son, if I say you are!" The squire glared at his eldest, who stared back at him. "And since you came home, as I wrote you. . . ."

"Wrote me? I came to see Theo's mistress." He glanced at Molly, a warm gleam in his eyes. "And she's been worth the trip."

The squire glared at him. "What!—you've not come here to beg my pardon?"

"For what? Though I may well have to beg Theo's pardon, for if he doesn't want his little cook, I'll—"

"Cook!" the squire thundered. Turning, he glared at Molly now. "You're a cook?"

She started to nod and answer, but Theo said, "Blazes, that's not to the point. And you—" he thrust out a finger at his brother. "Are to keep your hands off her. You don't have to run off with every female you see just to prove you can, for you only end up leaving them someplace anyway."

"Only the ones that bore me."

"Which ones don't! You're a worse jade than any I've met in London!"

Terrance scowled at his brother. "Do you want to finish what you started in the stable yard?"

"Anytime!"

The squire stepped forward, his voice raised. "You're not brawling in my house—I'll thrash the two of you, if you try it. And now what's all this about no letter and her being a cook?"

For a moment the room remained silent, then Theo folded his arms and said, voice calm, "I wanted to get disinherited so you'd have to take Terrance back. So I hired a . . . a cook to act like a strumpet and make a fool of you."

"Only you didn't know she was a cook 'til today, did you?" Terrance said.

Theo shot him a smoldering look, but it was the squire who demanded, "And you, sir, what do you mean you had no letter? How'd you know about her otherwise?"

Terrance shrugged. "There were plenty in London keen to tell me about Theo being seen driving out of town with her—and with my bays," he added, voice dropping to a threatening tone.

The squire threw his arm out and pointed to the doorway. "Well, then take your damn horses and go if you've not come home to reform your disgraceful behavior."

Terrance stiffened, but Theo stepped forward. "We are not all going to go through this again. Father, you know full well that you want to disown him about as much as you wish to cut off your foot. And Terrance, if you turn sullen and walk out, I swear I'll follow you and hound you until you turn and face your responsibilities!"

The squire and Terrance turned to stare at Theo as if he had broken out in green spots and a tail. Molly gave a silent cheer. Finally, someone in this family was talking sense instead of yelling.

Then the squire's face reddened. "And you, you— bringing home a . . . a . . . a whatever she is, playing your May-games! You may also consider yourself no longer part of this family!"

Theo's mouth thinned, Terrance turned on his father and looked ready to do him physical harm, and Molly's temper snapped. She had had enough.

Stepping into the middle of the three Winslows, she put her hands on her hips and glared at them. They all seemed surprised to have her in the midst of them, almost as if they had forgotten her presence.

"Look at yourselves. Just stop a moment and look! A father throwing his sons away—brothers who'd as soon pummel each other as draw a breath—and all of you, tearing what ought to be a family into no more than ill-feelings that are just hateful. I'm an orphan, and you make me glad of it! For when I came here, I thought this a fine house and those inside it rich."

"But you live in poverty, the lot of you. For there's more love to be squeezed from sour lemons than from any of you."

The squire started to mutter, but Molly rounded on him before he could speak, coming up to him and standing right before him, her face pushed close to his.

"You—you want your sons' respect, then show them some. They aren't boys. They aren't lads. They're grown men. And they have feelings that can be hurt—worse by you than by anyone. So isn't it time you stopped feeling sorry for yourself for how you were left alone—for you're not. You've two sons who need and love you."

That drew a snort from Terrance, so she turned on him, her face still hot and her veins singing, and while he held his ground as she advanced towards him, his chin dropped and he gave her a sullen look.

"And don't you think yourself better than your father, for you're just like him in that you think only of yourself. Only that's not made you happy, now has it?"

He started to answer, but she cut him off, ruthless and furious still. "Of course it hasn't—happiness isn't about drinking 'til you rot your guts with it, and you won't find it by taking everything and giving nothing. No, you learn fast on the lowest of London's streets that taking leaves a hole inside you that only makes you want to take more—only this life is about giving. Even a beggar in India knows that much!"

Breathing fast now, she turned to stare at Theo. What did she say to him? That it should not matter if she was a prostitute or a cook for a house of them? That what ought to matter was that she loved him?

Yes, that truth was out before her now, stark and bare.

But there was only one hope for it. One faint hope.

And it would be the hardest thing she had ever done, to do this right—and take that chance.

Why did she have to be born for a reckless life? And a reckless man, she hoped.

Turning around, she glared at the three men, now sulky and silent.

"You're all throwing away the most precious gifts—each other. And maybe that's what you need to do. Maybe you need to feel how empty the world is with no one to love you, or to love. Maybe you'd rather have your hard pride and your cold anger. I'm only a cook in a bawdy house, right enough, but I've nothing but pity for the lot of you!"

Head up, she walked out then.

She had to stop at the door for a last glance at Theo. "I always knew I wouldn't do for you." She looked at his family, then back to him. "And this won't do for me, either!"

She strode up to her room then, and threw her clothes into her trunk before yanking the bell, her stomach churning. No one came to stop her. Theo didn't come after her. And the hall was empty as a footman carried her trunk to the front door.

She stopped there, the hall quiet around her.

Then Simpson came forward. "I brought the shooting cart round for you," he said.

She glanced at him, eyes stinging. *God, don't let the tears spill now, please*, she prayed. She nodded, then glanced up the empty stairs and swallowed the hard lump.

"Thanks—ducks."

He bowed. "A pleasure, Miss Sweet. We'll miss you."

That did for her. She could bear with scorn, with hard words, with anger—she had done that all her life. But she had come to like these people, and even to respect the stiff, proper Simpson. Now, the softening in his glance, the sympathy in his voice, the regret that mirrored her own caught at her.

She tried not to sniffle; tried to keep some dignity and her already faltering hope. But she couldn't do that and meet his stare.

She couldn't say anything as she turned and found her way to the cart.

Someone gave her an open umbrella and she hunched under it as rain pelted down.

As the cart moved forward, she did not look back at Winslow Park.

She had not looked back from the ship at India, either.

Fifteen

What did a disowned son do? Theo wondered. He could ask Terrance he supposed, but just now he didn't want to talk to Terrance. Didn't want to talk to anyone.

From upstairs, he had watched Molly drive away in the shooting cart—a slight figure, a flash of red hair and striped dress, and then she disappeared into the rain and dimming light.

Should he ride after her? Should he not?

Blazes, but she'd heaped nothing but scorn on them all—and they had deserved it.

Only a cook. He'd give a good deal just now to be only a cook and not a damn Winslow.

But he was—or at least he was in name, if not by rights. Or he had been. *Oh, blazes take it all!*

Settling back in the straw of his favorite hunter's stall, he nursed a swallow from the bottle of brandy by his side and let it go hot and stinging down his throat.

After watching Molly leave, he had fled the house. With his jacket collar turned up and his head aching and feeling numb inside, he had gone to the stables where the horses didn't ask questions or do more than nudge a pocket, looking for a carrot or sliver of apple. He didn't need the brandy he had brought with him for more numbness. No, he was hoping it might instead clear that fog that swirled in his head.

What does a disowned son do?

What did he do about Molly?

George stirred in the stall, snuffled the brandy and then turned back to his hay. Theo let out a frustrated breath.

Truth was, it had been something of a relief to hear that she never had sold her body. He had known, in a way, that she wasn't a real harlot—or at least he could tell himself that. But blazes, couldn't she have told him before today? And why the hell did it rankle so much? Why did it still dig into him so much that it had kept him from going after her at once?

Or was it those last words?—*this won't do for me, either.*

He glanced at the brandy and rubbed his thumb across the brown glass. The harsh fumes mixed with the sweet scent of straw.

It wouldn't do for her. Well, she didn't have to settle for a life here. And a disowned son might marry a cook—might he not? But which of his friends would welcome him, then? And how could he take her off to the gambling hells he'd once thought would support him? Oh, devil take it, she didn't even want him.

And he could see why she wanted quits from this family.

He almost did himself.

Grimly, he smiled, for he half-wished he could blame this all on Terrance. However, he had put himself firmly into this disaster. He'd hired her in the first place.

He'd lost his head over her.

The stable door creaked and Theo glanced up, wondering if one of the grooms had seen the light of his lantern and come to check. Then he saw his father and he started to scramble to his feet.

"Sit down, la—sit down, Theo," the squire said, and Theo sat, a little shocked by the deep lines on his father's face. And then even more alarmed when the squire sat down in the straw next to him.

George came over and snuffled the squire's hair, and the squire reached up to pat the gelding's leg.

Not knowing what else to do, Theo offered the brandy.

The squire glanced at it, then shook his head. "No, I came to say something to you and that'll only make me forget it."

Theo nodded as if this actually made sense. Was this where his father tossed him from the Winslow lands and told him not to come back? If so, his father seemed remarkably reluctant. And quiet in going about it.

That left Theo uneasy.

"Quite the spitfire, your . . . your. . . ."

"My cook?" Theo suggested, the words bitter, though he had not intended them to come out so harsh.

The squire glanced at him and frowned. "Your Molly."

"She isn't mine. She has wisely taken herself back to London—or at least Simpson said she'd asked to be driven to the nearest posting house or stage inn." Theo raised the brandy. "To Molly in London, and her happiness."

The squire scowled. "Are you drunk?"

"I wish I were." Theo let out a sigh, then met his father's stare. "We put on quite a show for her, did we not?"

Glum, the squire nodded. Then he sat straighter. "I'm not used to some slip of a girl shaming me with her words—maybe I ought to be. I have thought of you two as my boys—my lads. For too long, it seems. I . . . I don't think I wanted you grown up and going off to live your own lives."

"So you send us away?"

The squire grumbled and plucked at the straw underneath him. Then he looked up. "Better to send you away than have you walk out. Like your mother did."

Theo sat very still. Had he drunk too much brandy? "My mother?"

"She . . . well, she didn't die. Not physically, least that

I know. But she left. So I buried an empty box. Told me she couldn't stand my temper. And I . . . I let my pride hold me, let it keep me from swearing I'd change, and I vowed not to instead. Hard, your Molly called it. It's that and more—unbearably hard. And it's been the regret of my life."

Theo stared at his father and tried to take in what had just been said. Nearby, George munched his hay, a soft sound. The rain beat on the cobbles in the stable yard and drafts of cold air slipped from the outside with a reminder that the warmth inside came from the horses.

Frowning, Theo finally managed to ask, "So she's alive?"

The squire shook his head. "To my shame—I don't know if she is still. She left me to live with her people, and I . . . I could not show my face to them. She may be. I never divorced her. Never would, though she wrote me once to say she'd not contest it."

He sat silent a moment, staring at the old hunter who shared the stall with them. "I still miss her."

Theo leaned back against the wood of the stall, comforting and solid behind him, for the rest of his world spun in his mind as if he had drunk the entire bottle of brandy. His mother. Alive. She had walked out on them all. Left her boys and her husband. Blazes, but life must have been worse than terrible for her to do that.

He glanced at his father, at the ragged lines worn into his face and the droop to his mouth and the hurt clouding his eyes.

What did one say?

The squire looked up, his mouth firming. "Do you love her?"

Theo blinked.

"Your Molly," the squire said.

Panic started inside Theo. Love seemed an enormous word. Then he made himself think on it.

Warmth spread through him as he thought of holding

her, of her laugh, of how irritating she could be with her questions, and how delighted she had looked the first time she had sat a trot without bouncing. His sweet Sweet. The woman who'd duped him.

"She's a cook!"

"And she makes a damn fine panda, but that wasn't the question," the squire said, irritable.

Theo frowned and struggled to be honest. If his father could confess that his mother was still alive—where in heavens?—he could return the truth. At last he said, "I don't know."

The squire rose stiff to his feet, then said, voice gruff, "Best find out, lad." He added, his tone softening, "I ought to be proud I raised sons who don't need anyone else to order their lives, but I'll still give you advice—pride ain't only hard, it's a damn poor bedfellow."

He put a hand on Theo's shoulder, and then let himself out of the stall.

Theo sat there, thoughts and feelings churning.

His mother. Alive.

God, this must be how Molly felt, wondering if somewhere in England she had someone who might love her and miss her as much as she wanted to love that someone.

And with that his mind began to turn.

"Those egg whites was done five minutes past—you beating them into cement?" Edna asked.

Molly stopped her whisk and then pushed a stray curl back with her wrist. She glanced at the egg whites. They were meant for meringues, but had gone past being stiff peaks. She had beaten the moisture out of them.

Distressed, she glanced at Edna, feeling the tears ready to tear loose again. She pushed them back. It had only been a fortnight since she had left Winslow Park, but it seemed years. She'd let go the faint hope that

Theo would come after her. He hadn't. Now she forced a smile. "We'll just have to start fresh," she said.

Edna gave a nod and took Alice with her to go back to the street stalls for more eggs, leaving Molly to pull herself together.

Sitting down on one of the high-backed wooden chairs, Molly put her forehead in her hand and rubbed. She had to stop thinking about Theo, stop this wondering about his family, stop these wretched "if onlys."

At least, after that first night back, Sallie had not asked a question nor said a thing.

There had been the start of a dreadful argument between them, when Molly came back with what was left of her ten pounds in her pocket after she had bought her ticket to London on the Bath mail coach.

Sallie had started in on her, asking what she was thinking not getting her payment, demanding to know what had happened.

And Molly hadn't been able to take one more argument.

She had turned and started to walk out the door.

Sallie had grabbed her shoulders and pulled her back in, taking her to the kitchen and ordering tea, and rubbing her hands.

She had said nothing more.

And Molly had said nothing about the fifty pounds Sallie had had from Theo.

That put them even, she figured. A paid holiday Sallie had once called it. Well, it had been that. And a good lesson, too.

She knew now that the reason she'd never had a beau wasn't due to her being too particular. She had been terrified to let anyone get close. She'd lost her parents, her uncle, and then had been left unclaimed on the docks, and she'd lost her first real friends in that fire, as well. And looking at Sallie's house now, she saw what a safe world she had made for herself—friends with a madam who knew how to keep her heart under lock and key, and living in a house where love and smiles were sold for a good price.

She'd made herself into one of those hard women without even having the physical pleasure in it—for now she had an idea just how much pleasure a man's body could give a woman.

Oh, she had kept herself safe, and all without even realizing it. Until she saw the Winslows doing the same thing—pushing love away.

Well, she was done with that.

She was already looking for an inn for sale at a price she could afford. And the next gentleman who took an interest in her, well, she'd take an interest, too.

But it would take some time to forget Theo. And that faint hope she'd had. A good long time.

Sitting up straight, she put back her shoulders. Well, no sense dragging over more "if onlys." What was done, was done. And if he couldn't see his way to her now, well. . . .

The tears stung her eyes again, and she got up to cut onions even though she didn't need any cut. It helped to have some excuse to cry.

"Coo, you're early in the day for a bit o' sport!"

Sallie glanced into the entry hall to see Barbara leaning over the stair railing, blond curls tousled, and her almost falling out of her dress as she smiled at a dark-haired man who had a book tucked under his arm and his hat in his hand. Odd, that book, but Sallie started forward, her own smile in place, ready to do business.

Then she heard his voice, low and pleasing. "Sorry— I'm partial to redheads."

He turned, and Sallie bore down on him. Blue eyes or

no. Fine shoulders or not. No gentlemen trifled with her girls. Not even with her cook.

"You're not welcome here, Mr. Theodore Winslow," she said, arms folded and glaring at him.

Cool as could be, he lifted his eyebrows and she hesitated about calling the two prize fighters she paid to keep order in her house. Then he pulled out a fat purse from the tail pocket of his coat, and her anger with him eased.

A heart might lead one to disaster—she knew it had for her Molly, poor mite—but, still, he'd come after her, he had. That might be a good sign.

And weren't those just the longest black eyelashes he had?

She took his arm to lead him into her parlor. "Molly won't see you, you know."

He didn't budge, but stayed rooted where he was. She had to let go his arm. She also began to reconsider. This wasn't the young gent who had come to her earlier this summer—no, he'd become a far more interesting flash fellow. Blue eyes stared down at her, something fixed in them.

"She'll see me. I've an account to settle with her, after all." A smile crooked his mouth at last. "So where's your kitchen and how much for an hour with her?"

Sixteen

At the sound of boots on the stairs, Molly looked up from dabbing the onion-tears from her cheeks with her apron.

It wasn't Tuesday, so it couldn't be Mr. Goslin come to fill the milk pitchers.

Then Theo stepped into the room and she stared at him, thinking herself a disaster and that she'd never seen anything so wonderful in her life as him. Even with him in dusty boots and breeches and a shadow of beard darkening his jaw.

She pulled in a breath, then let it out with her words, "Hello, ducks."

He came forward, putting a book down on the kitchen table. Molly gripped her apron tighter to keep herself from flinging her arms about him. She wasn't sure just where they stood with each other.

After glancing around, he looked at her. "I bought an hour with you."

She straightened and dropped her apron. "My time's no longer for sale."

Mischief glinted in his eyes. "You should tell Sallie that."

She glared at him. "How much now?"

"Less than what I owe you." Theo tossed a leather pouch on the table. Coins clattered as the pouch hit the wood. He shouldn't tease her this way, but after spending so much time on her behalf, he couldn't resist tormenting her a little. She had done nothing but haunt his dreams.

And, with his mouth dry and his palms damp, he needed time to gauge her reactions. She'd looked delighted at first to see him, but then she'd gone wary on him. Blazes, but did she really have nothing but scorn for him and his family?

If she did, he'd change that. It was why he'd come prepared.

She didn't move to touch the money, but stepped over to the other end of the table and picked up a long-handled wooden spoon to stir what looked like a bowl of white fluff. "You don't owe me a thing."

"Don't I just? Well, if you don't want coins—what about this?" He flipped open the book. Then he waited. Would she take the bait? She must. She was always curious about everything.

If she didn't, he vowed he'd simply walk over and kiss her senseless. Only that wouldn't really solve anything between them. No, they had to talk this out. And he hated that.

But, for her, he'd do it.

She eyed him warily, but came closer, that wooden spoon in her hand held up like a sword. Then, as she read, leaning close but not touching the page, her jaw slackened. Finally she looked up at him, her eyes starting to glow. "It's about my father."

Theo's shoulders relaxed. This would work. It had to work. "Captain David Sweet of the King's Thirty-Third, there's more, but I thought you might like to read it yourself rather than have me tell you about it."

She stared at him, her expression puzzled. "And this is all you came to London for?"

With a smile, he snagged her arm, the one that held the wooden spoon. "No, that's not all I've come to London for."

She tried to pull back, but he already had hold of her apron strings. She slapped his hand away, but he shifted strategy and plucked the cap from her curls, tossing the white lace aside. She had on a white dress with a yellow scarf knotted about her neck and he was already wondering if it all tied up in front—handy for a fellow, that.

"I hate caps," he said. "Come to think of it, I hate bonnets, too, or anything else that covers that glorious hair of yours."

Molly's cheeks warmed. "It's not fair your talking like that."

"Why not?"

"Because I'm not able to think sensible when you do!"

He grinned. "And it's important to think sensible?"

"With you it is."

Letting go of her, he put his hands behind his back. "That better?"

Molly tried to retie her apron, but her fumbling hands managed to tangle it with the spoon. Letting out a frustrated breath, she tossed the spoon aside and tore off the apron. "No, it is not better—here you come waltzing in, saying you've bought an hour of my time and I don't know why you're here or what—"

"I'm here because I couldn't stay away."

She stared up at him, heart beating faster. "Oh."

He stepped closer. "And I would have come sooner, only I didn't want to show up empty handed." She glanced at the leather pouch on the table, but he reached out and turned her chin so that she had to look at him. "Not to bring you money, my Molly-may."

She held utterly still, shocked. "What did you call me?"

His mouth crooked, then he dug into his waistcoat and pulled out a folded letter. "Molly-may—it's what your uncle called you."

Hands trembling, she took the letter and unfolded it to scan the lines. She recognized the scrawl at once, even though it had been years. Her uncle's hand—or at least, how it had been after the fever had him and he could barely write.

"Where did you get this?" she asked. Then she looked up at Theo, excitement bubbling in her. "Lady Thorpe? She is my aunt!"

Theo shook his head. But at her dismay, he gave up teasing. "Not your aunt—your godmother. She and her sister, Amy, seem to have been neighbors and best-of-friends with your mother, Amelia, and her sister. I think there's a blood tie of some sort but I couldn't wade through all that. But she had that letter tucked in her Bible—it came to her through your mother's sister who didn't dare defy her family and go to meet you herself. And I'd wager, your family were the kind souls who also disclaimed knowledge of your mother and father!"

"But she never did—meet me, I mean. Oh, gracious, was she ill even then and forgetting?"

With a shake of his head, he gestured to the letter. She looked again and saw a torn section of newspaper as he said, "Look what ship is circled."

She glanced at the paper—it gave the names of the East India merchant ships docking in London. "The *Armiston*? But I sailed on the *Carmathen*."

Her cheeks paled and she looked again at her uncle's letter. She wanted to sit down then. It had all been a mistake. A dreadful mistake. The wrong ship met, for with her uncle's scrawling hand, even she could barely make out the proper name of the ship.

Then she looked up at Theo. At least it had come right—years late, but not too late. "I'm her goddaughter, you said?"

He grinned and nodded.

With a scowl, she pushed the papers at him. "I suppose that makes me tolerable now! So that's why you could bear to come to see me. Well, you may just take yourself off again!"

Turning, she stalked around the table, intent on leaving, her cheeks burning. Of course he hadn't wanted her when she was just a cook in a bawdy house. But did he have to come to her now that he thought her nearly acceptable and tempt her with himself?

He rounded the table before her and placed himself between her and the door. "I've not had my full hour yet! And I've not had what I came for—which is you, my sweet Sweet."

"Oh, stop calling me that."

"Then what should I call you?" he asked, advancing towards her. "My Molly-may? My delight? I've come to London for you and I'm not leaving without you."

"Why?" she demanded, hands on her hips.

He stopped and blinked at her. "Why what?"

"Why have you come for me and why do you want me? Is it because you think I'm almost respectable now that I have Lady Thorpe for a godmother?"

"Of course not! Blazes, as if I would!"

"Well, then why?"

He glared at her. "You're going to make me say this, aren't you?"

She let out a sigh and rolled her eyes. "Of course I am. I spent enough time with you Winslows to see how you like to keep unsaid all the things you ought to be saying—you expect everyone to just 'know.' Well, I want more. I want to hear you say for yourself why you—"

"Because I love you, damn it!"

She stared at him, then began to smile. "You do?"

"Of course I do!" In two strides he had hold of her hands. "Why else would I spend all that time with Lady Thorpe—enough, I may say, that Bedlam was starting to seem a nice place to visit! I wanted to bring you something—something you'd value. And I couldn't

think what you'd want more than to know that someone tried to meet you—that someone wanted you."

"Oh, Theo!"

His eyes darkened. "I want you as well."

She stared up at him, trembling inside, feeling as she
had years ago on the London docks with an unknown
world waiting for her. "I—I want you as well. But you
can't marry a cook who dreams of owning an inn."

"And why can't I? Buy your inn, if you like. Blazes, buy
a dozen of them—Lady Thorpe'll probably leave you
enough for it. Or make your own fortune by writing one
of those fat books on cookery like that one that jeweler's
widow put out."

"What do you know about cookery books?"

"I'll have you know that I know a good deal—Sylvain
Harwood's sister married a fellow who prints books. Po-
etry mostly, and Sylvain's forever saying they make
nothing on them, and keeps telling them to put out
books on animals, travel or cooking." He grinned. "I like
the thought of *Domestic Cookery* by Mrs. Winslow?"

"Mrs.—?"

His grin widened and he pulled her into his arms.
"Yes, Mrs. Winslow, if that's your wish. Marry me, or be
my mistress—whatever suits your fancy. I'm the one
who's unworthy of you—you said it yourself that we
wouldn't suit. But I want us to. For I like how you fit in
my arms. And—well, before you came along, I had no
idea what love even was, or how it was lacking in my own
life. I don't want to lose that—I don't want to lose you.
So what must I do to have you?"

She stared up at him, wanting to believe in this and in
him, and half-afraid of it. But hadn't she just promised
herself that with the first fellow who showed interest,
she'd find the interest, too?

Still, she had to settle one thing more.

"But with my past—what of the scandal? And I won't come between you and your father!"

He tightened his hold on her. "You won't—he swears you make an excellent panda. Just what in blazes is a panda?"

"It's a drink—and why did he say that?"

"Because he just about told me I'd best come and fetch you back. I'm not the only Winslow you've enslaved. I think he might even curb his temper a little for you—but only a very little, so don't get your hopes up there. But I do fancy having a wife who looks lovely with flour on her cheek."

She put a hand to brush at her face. It came away clean. "I haven't, you wretch!"

"Then let's put some there." With a wink he turned her, pushing aside bowls as he lay her down on the kitchen table.

She gave a laugh, then said, nearly breathless, "Theo, you can't!"

"I can—my hour's not gone, and Sallie promised me I'd not be disturbed. Besides, you wanted scandal."

"I didn't!"

"You did—you said 'what of it?' And it's best you get accustomed to it now anyway, for don't you know by now that the Winslows are always the talk of the neighborhood."

"You are a wretch," she said as he began to nuzzle her neck. Then she let out a sigh and her eyes drifted closed with the pleasure of it—of him.

"Yes, I am," he muttered just before his lips found hers.

And then he settled in to show her just how scandalous a Winslow really could be.

AUTHOR'S NOTE

In the era of sailing ships it could indeed be tricky to know the exact day a ship might dock. Passenger lists, too, were not always regularly kept, so it seemed quite possible that a girl, without someone to claim her, could vanish into the workhouses of Regency England.

Researching the food and recipes for this book was a much brighter spot and I'm indebted to two main sources—an 1814 edition of *Domestic Cookery* by Mrs. Maria Rundell and *The Art of Cookery Made Plain and Easy* by Hanna Glass, published in 1765. Mrs. Rundell, the widow of one of the famous jewelers of the Regency era—Rundell and Bridges—included in her book not just recipes but menus, advice for dealing with servants, and wonderful household tips, such as how to dye white gloves a beautiful purple and to prevent the rot in sheep. Amazing what a woman had to know.

As for prostitution during the Regency, it had grown right along with London's population; there were guides to brothels and to the various women for hire. Such activities were illegal. However, since there was no organized police force (Sir Robert Peel's peelers or Bobbies came along in 1829), it was difficult for the law to keep up with enforcing any sort of morality, which included illegal gambling, boxing, and other forms of vice.

In the Regency, really, it was not so much what you did, as that you did it with style and discretion. Which is why it was not so much that Terrance ran off with the vicar's daughter that upset his father, it was that he made it into a public disaster by abandoning her and was not the least repentant. Since a daughter was considered a father's property, a father could sue for damages to his daughter's person and reputation, as well as for breech of contract if a marriage was promised and not fulfilled. Terrance being Terrance wouldn't give a hang about such details—and all that's going to get him in even more trouble in his story, *Barely Proper,* a title which pretty well sums up his character.

I do enjoy hearing from readers, so write or e-mail, and don't forget to ask for a free bookmark: Shannon Donnelly, P.O. Box 3313, Burbank, CA 91508-3313, read@shannondonnelly.com.

More Zebra Regency Romances